PROTECTING MARIA (SPECIAL FORCES: OPERATION ALPHA)

Guardian Seals: Book 2

NICOLE FLOCKTON

Dear Readers,

Welcome to the Special Forces: Operation Alpha Fan-Fiction world!

If you are new to this amazing world, in a nutshell the author wrote a story using one or more of my characters in it. Sometimes that character has a major role in the story, and other times they are only mentioned briefly. This is perfectly legal and allowable because they are going through Aces Press to publish the story.

This book is entirely the work of the author who wrote it. While I might have assisted with brainstorming and other ideas about which of my characters to use, I didn't have any part in the process or writing or editing the story.

I'm proud and excited that so many authors loved my characters enough that they wanted to write them into their own story. Thank you for supporting them, and me!

READ ON!
Xoxo
Susan Stoker

ABOUT THE BOOK

This book was previously published in Amazon Kindle Worlds

She'd thought she'd left her old life behind. She was wrong.

Surgical resident Maria Moretti's life is finally becoming her own, that is until her past catches up with her and she is forced to operate on her uncle. Normally, saving a loved one isn't a problem, unless you're related to one of the most notorious mob families in New York. Now, the family Maria's distanced herself from is doing everything they can to bring her back into the fold.

Former Navy SEAL turned security expert, Riley

"Ash" Ashland, is reluctant to take on the job of protecting Maria. That is, until he meets her. Seeing how much she wants her freedom from the stranglehold her family has on her changes his mind. Even though she refuses to believe she needs protection, Riley watches over her. When her life is threatened, he calls on all his resources to keep her safe. But can he protect his heart at the same time?

Can Maria keep from dragging Riley into her twisted mob world while she fights for her independence all over again?

ACKNOWLEDGMENTS

Thank you Susan Stoker for allowing me to be part of your awesome Kindle World. It was hard to choose from all your characters which ones to put in my story.

To Wren Michaels for bugging me, well encouraging me, to take the plunge and dive into the world of SEALs. Have to say it was well worth it!

As always I have a wonderful cover because of Jennifer from More Than Words Promotions. Thank you for working your magic again, and for everything else you do for me.

To the readers of Susan's world—I really hope you

enjoy Riley and Maria's story. Thank you for making me feel so welcome and taking the time to one click my story.

Finally, to my family, you truly are the best.

DEDICATION

To Susan Stoker & her Readers – thank you for letting me be part of your world.

CHAPTER ONE

Maria twisted the knot until it tightened and held before snipping the fine, silky black thread. Sweat trickled down her spine. The fact her hands remained steady was only due to her determination not to let the bastards know they were getting to her.

She threw the suture needle into the metal kidney shaped dish, the small tool joining the three bullets she'd extracted. "There it's done."

The removal of the gun barrel that had been held against her head for the last two hours should've been a relief. Only it wasn't. Maria Moretti knew, after tonight, the life she'd spent the last ten years working hard to create was over. Her past had found her and she knew it wouldn't let her go.

"Very good, Dr. Moretti. I'm sure Uncle Vittorio is very grateful that you saved his life."

The sleaze ball who snatched her out of the hospital parking lot was far too smug for her liking.

"Like I had a choice," she muttered and snapped off her latex gloves. "Now, how about you and your goons, take my Uncle and get the hell away from me. I don't want anything to do with him or the family anymore. My father knows this. And if you happen to see my loser of a father, give him the following message." She glared at sleaze ball, waiting until he nodded. "Stay the fuck out of my life. Like he promised he would."

Without waiting for a response of any kind, she grabbed her bag and walked out of the dirty, drafty doctor's surgery they'd taken her to. Having been bundled in the back of a windowless van, she had no idea where in the city she was. But this was New York; if she walked a couple of blocks she'd find a cab or a subway station. All she needed to do was get as far away from this place as possible. God, she hoped this would be the last time she'd see anyone from her mob family again. Somehow she didn't think she was going to be so lucky.

A loud banging on her apartment door jolted Maria from her sleep. A quick glance at her bedside clock and the green luminous numbers showed six a.m.

Who the hell knocking on her front door at this time of the morning?

Throwing back the covers she made her way toward the door. "I'm coming," she yelled at whoever was on the other side of her wooden door pounding loud enough to wake the dead. Her neighbors were going to love her for their early morning wake up call.

After the night she'd had there was no way she was going to unlatch the chain and disengage the locks. She may be sleepy, but no one ever said Maria Moretti didn't have any street smarts. It was a damn pity exhaustion had had her off her game last night. If she'd been more aware, she may not have found herself in the situation she ended up in.

"Who's there?" she asked.

"FBI, Ma'am. Open up please."

FBI? What the fuck?

Of course, it could be a trick. If the goon from last night had passed on her message to dear old dad, she wouldn't put it past him pull a trick like this on her.

Maria twisted the locks and opened the door until the chain caught. "Show me your badge?"

A second later a meaty looking hand protruded through the door holding out a leather pouch with a glittering gold badge and the name *Agent Scott Whittaker* typed neatly beside the FBI emblem.

Everything looked legit. But looks could be deceiving. She didn't think that was the case this time though. Maria suspected the early morning visit was connected to the out of the way surgery she performed last night.

After so many years of freedom she'd thought it was safe to stop looking over her shoulder. Last night proved she'd always have to look.

She had no choice—again. If she refused their entry, they'd only force their way in.

"Watch your hand," she commanded as she pushed the door shut and disengaged the chain.

Maria held the door open and three men dressed in suits walked in. Who the hell wore suits at six in the morning?

Her normally spacious looking foyer seemed tiny with three large men taking up the space. Manners took over. "Why don't we go into the living room and you can tell me why you needed to almost breakdown my door this early in the morning?"

The man whose badge she read spoke. "As I

showed you. I'm Agent Whittaker," he then pointed to the man to his right. "This is Agent Williams and this is Agent Clements." He canted his head to the left. "We're sorry to disturb you so early, Dr. Moretti, but we believe you have some information that could help us with a case."

Her stomach plummeted as her suspicions were confirmed. No way was she going to let the Feds know she had an idea why they were visiting. Adopting her concerned doctor face she lifted her chin and looked Agent Whittaker in the eye. "I'm not sure what you're talking about."

Whittaker's eyebrows rose a fraction. "Can you confirm that you are the daughter of Giovanni Moretti, currently residing in New Jersey? Also the suspected leader of the Moretti Mafia."

And there it was. The name she'd sworn never to think of again after she'd walked out of the monstrosity that had been her home and headed to college. Her father had agreed to release her from any familial obligations. Until he needed a surgeon, of course, and then he used her. Why did she have to be working the night Uncle Vittorio got shot? Actually, it probably wouldn't have mattered if she hadn't been working. Dear old papa would've taken her from her house. She wasn't stupid enough to think he didn't know where she lived. The irony of her moving to

New York to do her surgical residency wasn't lost on
her. If she'd had any sense she would've gone to a
West Coast Hospital.

"Ms. Moretti? I didn't think my question was that
difficult to answer."

No, not difficult, just admitting out loud what she
was trying hard to forget wasn't easy. No matter how
much she tried, she knew it was impossible. How
could you forget your heritage? No matter how
bloody that heritage was.

"Yes. I am Giovanni Moretti's daughter."

"Are you a surgical resident at Bridgedale Hospital
in Brooklyn?"

"Yes."

"Did you perform an unscheduled surgery last
night in a non-hospital environment?"

How the fuck did they know about that? She was
in a no win situation: lying to federal agents could
have her spending time in jail. If she told the truth,
the family she longed to forget would come after her.
Either option would put her career in jeopardy, and
she'd be damned if she'd lose everything she'd worked
the last ten years to achieve.

Shit, she hated her family for dragging her back
into their snake pit.

"May I remind you Ms. Moretti, lying to a federal
agent will land you in serious trouble."

"I'm aware of that. Yes, I performed a surgery last night."

Agent Whittaker scribbled something in his notebook, and then looked back at her. "Are you permitted to perform surgeries away from the hospital? You're still a resident aren't you?"

Memories of the previous evening burst to life in her mind in all its technicolor glory. "You know, when you get snatched off your feet as you're walking to your car, shoved into the back of a van, and taken to some hole in the wall facility to perform surgery on a man you haven't seen in a decade. All while being held at gunpoint, you don't have time to say—*hey I'm a fourth year surgical resident. I'm not supposed to be performing surgeries unsupervised just yet*—all I was thinking about was keeping myself alive."

She hadn't meant to reveal so much but once the words started she couldn't stop them.

Agent Whittaker made a couple more notes before he stood. "I think that's all we need at the moment." He reached into his pocket and pulled out a slim black folder. He extracted a card and handed it to her. "I'll be in touch and if you need anything, and I mean *anything* at all, please call."

Maria took the card knowing full well there was no way she was going to contact the agent. She wanted nothing to do with the feds and she especially didn't want anything to do with her family.

A yawn ripped through Maria as she studied the case files for her up and coming surgeries. All pretty straight forward, nothing nearly as complicated as the one she'd performed the previous evening. Even under the less than sanitary circumstances, and without all the equipment she was used to having, she'd saved a life. The fact the life she'd saved didn't deserve to still be breathing today, annoyed the hell out of her. She'd honored her oath. An oath her father knew she wouldn't ignore, which was no doubt why he'd tracked her down.

Her pocket vibrated and she pulled out her phone and smiled when she saw Melody's name pop up.

"Hiya, Melody, how are you? How's Tex? And the girls?"

"Hey Maria. I'm good. Tex and the girls are great.

"I bet Hope is getting bigger with each day that passes. And I'm sure all she has to do is smile and Tex is putty in her hand."

Melody laughed loudly. "You have no idea. Hope is growing like a weed and, as for Tex, well sometimes

I swear he loves that girl more than me. He melts whenever Hope giggles or smiles at him."

"The big bad SEAL humbled by a toothless grin." Maria couldn't keep the jealousy out of her voice. She loved her career and was super proud of what she'd achieved. Except there was a hole in her life: she had no one special to share her milestones with. No one who put her first and made her weak at the knees like she knew Tex did to Melody.

"Oh, trust me, he's still the big bad SEAL and whenever I take the girls anywhere without him, he always checks the location and all routes to get to said destination. He always has eyes on us to makes sure the girls and I are safe."

If Tex had eyes on *her* maybe she wouldn't have been in this dilemma, but then again, why would Tex be interested in what she did or where she went.

"You're lucky, Mel. I need to come and visit you guys."

"Yes, you do. But," Melody's voice turned serious. "How are you doing? Is everything okay?"

Maria opened her mouth to spill her troubles, but held back. Melody was one of the few friends she had. With her family connections it was safer to keep a distance between any relationships she made. Even though Melody had Tex and a whole SEAL team looking out for her. When it came to the Mob, even the military couldn't penetrate their walls.

She couldn't expose Melody to the dangers of her family, no matter how much she wanted to talk to someone about everything that had happened to her in the last twenty-four hours.

"Everything's fine. I'm just tired, still working insane hours."

"Are you sure that's all?"

Maria had never told Melody about her Mob family. She'd met Melody when they'd both been vacationing in Philadelphia. Maria had been lost and Melody had helped her out. They'd been friends ever since. But still, Maria had been shocked when she'd found out that Melody had been stalked and Tex had rescued her.

"Yep, long hours and early wake up calls don't make for a very happy Maria."

"Look," Melody paused. "I know about your family, and if you need any help at all. Tex and I are here for you."

The words rushing out of Melody's mouth struck her speechless. She knew about her family? No, it was impossible. How could she know?

"What are you talking about?"

"Tex, being Tex, looked into your background. He did that with all my friends after the Diane incident."

Her stomach bottomed out at Melody's declaration—they knew she was the daughter of the head of the infamous Moretti Mob. And they hadn't breathed a word to her. "And he still let you remain friends with me?"

Melody chuckled. "I love Tex, but I also treasure my friends, I told him I didn't want to cut you off. I don't deny he had his doubts. I told him you'd never once given me any reason to be concerned about you. If you were as heartless as your father, you wouldn't be a surgeon saving lives."

"Thank you for your belief in me. I'm not sure I deserve it."

"Trust me, you more than deserve it. So, now that's out of the way, you wanna tell me what's really going on with you."

A colleague walked past reminding Maria she wasn't sitting in the privacy of her own home. She didn't want to say too much over the phone. After today she was off for the next three days, a very rare long weekend. Maybe a trip to Pennsylvania would be good for her. Give her some breathing space between what happened and the fallout from it.

"Are you up for a visitor?" Maria asked.

"You don't need to ask. When can we expect you?"

"I can be there tomorrow morning. I'll catch an

early train. I'll find a hotel and will call you once I get settled."

"You'll do no such thing. You can stay with us. And I'm not taking no for an answer and neither will Tex. Even with Hope, we've still got a spare room."

Maria knew arguing with Melody would be pointless. Plus she was too exhausted to argue. Knowing she had a friend who she could unburden herself to lightened the load on her shoulders.

"Great. I'll see you tomorrow. And Mel?"

"Yes?"

"Thanks."

"You're welcome, honey. Don't forget to text me all your details."

"I won't. Bye."

Ending the call, she put her phone beside her. A couple of days out of town was just want the doctor ordered. Lucky she was good at self-diagnosis.

CHAPTER TWO

Thank God it was Friday. It had been a hell of a week. After finalizing a particularly hairy surveillance job, Riley *Ash* Ashland, was looking forward to a quiet day.

Coffee in hand he opened the door to Warren & Ashland Security Services and headed toward his office.

"Lily, sweetheart, you don't need a birth plan."

Riley chuckled to himself as Grayson 'Storm' Warren's voice floated down the hallway.

"But Gray, the books all say, a birth plan is the way to go if you want to have your perfect birth."

Listening in on a conversation about birth plans wasn't quite how he wanted to start his morning. He reached Storm's office and poked his head through the open doorway.

"Morning, you two."

Storm looked up, exasperation written all over his face. Riley bit back a chuckle. He would've thought that after two years of marriage, he would've realized that Lily would have a list for a perfect birth. After all, she'd written a perfect man list. The fact Storm was the exact opposite of everything on her list, should've told Lily she couldn't make a list for everything.

"Riley, can you please tell Grayson that a birth plan is a good idea."

Riley held up his hands in surrender, his satchel slapped against his hip and he tightened his hold on his cup so his coffee didn't spill. "Oh no, leave me out of this. I'd never get in between a couple."

"Wuss, your loyalty should be to me, your friend, business partner and guy who had your back," Storm grumbled good-naturedly before rubbing a hand over his wife's protruding belly. An irrational twinge of longing swept over Riley. "Lily, babies don't come according to your schedule. They have their own. By all means make a plan, but be flexible."

"Sound advice, Lily," Riley agreed. Lily's death stare had him back tracking out of the office. "I'll be heading to my office now."

He made a quick getaway, chuckling to himself in an effort to dispel the unwelcome feeling he'd had while watching Lily and Storm together. One thing was for certain, it was nothing, if not entertaining, when Lily visited.

Opening his office door, he set his coffee on his desk before removing his bag to get his laptop out. Today would be catch up on all the paperwork to close out the case he'd been working on. It was never fun to confirm a husband's suspicion that not only was his wife was cheating on him, let alone when it was with the guy's best friend, she was also handing off information to his opposition making him lose contracts. Sometimes there were some cases he didn't like handling.

His cell phone vibrated on his desk, and he reached for it, smiling when he saw Tex's name pop up. They hadn't been on the same SEAL team when they'd been in the service together. In fact, he'd had more to do with Tex after they'd both left the military, than when they'd been in it. Tex had sent him some cases when he'd started his own PI business, and once he joined forces with Storm, they'd been getting a lot more work.

"Hey Tex, what's up?"

"Hey Ash, you got plans for this weekend?"

In all the time he'd known Tex, not once had he asked Riley if he had plans for the weekend.

"Not that I'm aware of. I've just finished a job so was planning on taking it easy. Why?"

"Think you can come to here?"

Tex was being very vague, which wasn't like him. He'd always been a straight up guy. That was one of the things he'd like about his friend.

"I might. If you want to tell me what's going on?"

"Mel had a call from a friend. We think she's in trouble and may need protection. The only thing is she's the type of girl who's going to object strongly about having anyone follow her."

Interest piqued, Riley sat a little straighter in his chair. "Any idea what kind of trouble she might have got herself into?"

"No idea, but my best guess is, it's something to do with her family. They're not the best sort."

"Tell me a family who is?" As an only child and with both his parents dead, Riley had no concept of happy families. He was a late in life baby and by the time he was eighteen he was an orphan. Joining the military had been a no brainer. It wouldn't matter if he died while in service. No one would miss him. If he'd died serving his country, he couldn't think of a more honorable way to go.

Now he had his former SEAL team as family and worked with Storm. Life had turned out pretty well for him.

"Let's just say, Maria's family is one you can never get away from. No matter how much you want to or think you can."

"Just tell me who her family is Tex. Stop avoiding the subject."

"Maria's dad is Giovanni Moretti."

"Fuck."

Anyone who worked in law enforcement or security of any type in New York City knew exactly who Giovanni Moretti was. Anyone with half a brain cell would keep the hell away from anyone associated with that family. You never wanted to be put on one of Giovanni's lists. Getting off them was near impossible.

"Yeah, that." Tex responded dryly.

"I'm not su—"

"Hear me out before you object."

"It's not just me I have to think about, Tex. Any job decisions are made jointly between me and Storm. With Lily pregnant I know he's not going to want to put her in any sort of danger."

"I get that, but Maria is one of the good ones. She's spent the last decade putting distance between her and her family. She's a fourth year surgical resident. From what I've found out she's a good one too."

Riley breathed in deeply. He didn't have plans for the weekend. He could check out the situation and then talk to Storm about it. He trusted Tex not to put him in a bad situation.

"Fine. I can come up and see you this weekend. I'm not promising we'll take the job on."

"That's all I need, Ash. Besides, knowing Maria, she's going to object to any kind of protection. Plus it could all be nothing."

Riley scoffed. "If it was nothing, you wouldn't be calling me, Tex."

"This is true. Can you get up here by tonight?"

"Yeah, as I mentioned, I finished a job yesterday so nothing pressing. I'll check in with Storm and then get on the road.

"Great, I know Mel said Maria could stay with us, so I'll make you a reservation at a nearby hotel."

"That'll work. See you in a few hours."

Riley disconnected the call and sat back in his chair. If it had just been him, he probably would take the job no questions asked. Now there were more people to think about. The Moretti's tentacles had a long reach and once they latched onto you, they never let go. There was a lot to consider.

He reached for his computer and searched up Maria Moretti's name. If he was going to do this, he planned on being prepared. He would dig up as much information on Maria as possible.

A few hours later Riley pulled into Tex's driveway. The trip from New York to Tex's place had passed without too much drama. He'd checked into the hotel and dumped his bags.

He hoped Maria hadn't arrived already. He wanted to talk to Tex about her. There hadn't been a lot of information about her online. Most of the articles had talked about her pursuing a medical career and trying to keep the distance between her and her father. His further digging hadn't uncovered a boyfriend or significant other. Seemed her life consisted of work, work and more work. Not surprising considering breaking into the medical field wasn't an easy task. Plus becoming a surgeon required even more dedication and patience.

The front door opened as Riley stepped out of the car. He grabbed his laptop bag from the trunk and made his way to where Tex stood on the front porch.

"Ash, good to see you. You made good time." Tex held out his hand and Riley grasped his.

"Good to see you too. Yeah surprisingly traffic wasn't too bad."

They walked inside and the scent of tomatoes and

garlic wafted to Riley, his stomach grumbling in appreciation.

Tex laughed. "I guess you didn't stop to grab some food on the way up."

"Well, if you can call a gas station tuna salad sandwich food, then yes I did."

"That's not food, that's taking your life in your own hands." The words were spoken by Melody, as she walked into the hallway, a fair-haired child on her hip. "Glad you could make it up here, Riley."

Riley leaned down and placed a kiss on Melody's cheek. "My pleasure. I take it your friend's not here yet?"

Melody shook her head. "Not yet. Her train should be arriving in about half an hour. Tex offered to get her but she said she'd get a cab."

"You let her catch the train and a cab. Why would you do that if there is a possible threat to her?" Riley asked. Surprised someone as cautious about the safety of others as Tex was would let Maria arrange her own transportation.

Tex laughed. "Maria didn't think we knew about her family. Of course, we did and so it was a shock for her to find out we knew who her father was. She's very independent and, as we don't know exactly what's up with her I figured I could give her some space. Besides, trying to talk her out of doing it would be impossible. I warn you, it's going to be a hard sell to get her to think about you protecting her."

Hearing the words spoken out loud, made Riley realize he'd already made the decision to take on the job. Even though it could prove to be extra dangerous to him and the firm. He knew Tex wouldn't want to protect Maria if she wasn't a good person. No way would he want to have someone associated with the Mob anywhere near his wife and family.

"Right. So how are we going to explain my presence here? I'm guessing you're not going to introduce me as Riley Ashford, your new bodyguard."

"No, we'll go with the truth. You're an ex-SEAL like me. The only place we'll fabricate the truth is the fact that we invited you up here, after speaking to her. We'll say you were in Ohio on business and called in for a visit on the way home."

"What the hell type of business would I be doing in Ohio? I mean a surveillance job isn't out of the realm of possibility. If we don't want her to know what I do, then we'll have to come up with something credible she'll believe."

"We could always say you're a traveling insurance salesman," Melody suggested.

Riley laughed at the suggestion. "How clichéd."

Melody shrugged and the baby on her hip started

to cry. "Oh that's my cue to get this little one a snack. Akilah will be home from school soon. You boys need to work out what story you're going with."

With that Melody left them where they still stood in the hallway. Riley watched as Tex tracked every sway of his wife's hips.

What would it be like to love someone that unconditionally? To trust another person to look after your heart and hope like hell they don't crush it. Storm and Lily had gone through a few difficulties, but were now on the way to becoming their own family. Lily's assistant and best friend Rita was included in the nucleus of their family.

The only time he'd felt anything closely resembling a family had been when he'd been a SEAL. He and Storm had been on the same team and even though he spoke to the guys, they never met up on a regular basis. Riley knew Tex had grown close to one particular SEAL team, helping the guys when their women were in trouble.

Maybe he should get in touch with Robot and the others when they were back stateside.

"Where'd you go, Ash?" Tex pulled him back from his thoughts.

Riley shrugged. "Just thinking I need to get in touch with the guys from my team. It's been too long since I've seen them."

"They'll be back in Virginia in a couple of weeks."

Riley knew better than to ask how Tex knew this information. The guy probably did more for the military now than he'd ever done when he'd been on a team.

"Good to know. I'll send Robot an email and wait to hear from him."

The chance to work on their cover story was lost when the doorbell rang. "Looks like your other guest is here."

Tex nodded. "Just follow my lead. We'll suss out Maria and go from there."

"Understood."

Riley moved to the side to let Tex past so he could open the door. With his gaze locked in on the piece of wood that shut them away from the outside world his first glimpse of Maria Moretti would be forever etched in his mind. Brown hair flowed over her shoulders like chocolate flowing over a fountain. He couldn't see her eyes but he imagined they would be a darker shade than her hair. The loose fitting white top she wore couldn't hide her curves. Her jeans clung tightly to her legs. He had no trouble picturing those legs wrapped around him.

He slammed the brakes on his train of thought.

No, he wasn't going to do a Storm and fall for the person he was protecting. No matter how attractive.

CHAPTER THREE

Relief coursed through Maria the second Tex's strong arms closed around her in a welcoming hug. Tension had been riding her shoulders the whole trip from New York to Pittsburgh. She'd lost count of how many times she looked over her shoulder to see if anyone was following her.

Her phone had been ominously quiet after the Feds had left apartment. She had been expecting someone from the family to call her. To find out if she'd spilled anything to the agents who'd interviewed her.

Could she hope that she was over-reacting and her dad would keep the promise about leaving her alone he'd made to her all those years ago? If that were the case, then why had Uncle Vittorio's goons pressured her into performing surgery on him? A request like that would've only come from her father.

"Stop thinking, you're safe here."

Tex's whispered words dumbfounded her. How had he known what was going through her mind? It didn't matter how he knew, all that mattered now was that she believed him. For the next forty-eight hours she could let her guard down. After that, well she was a big girl and she could handle whatever the Moretti family, and the Feds, threw at her.

"It's good to see you, Tex. It's been too long."

Tex released her and she walked into the house, stopping at the sight of a tall man standing in the middle of the hallway. His arms were crossed over his broad chest. Maria would estimate him to be as tall, or a couple of inches taller, than Tex. His dark hair was closely cropped to his skull. Standing in the shadows of the hallway she couldn't really make out his features. One thing she knew though, everything about him screamed military.

"Who are you?" The words burst out of her.

The stranger walked toward her, getting within a foot of her before stopping. She craned her neck a little to get a better look at his face, then wished she hadn't. His brown eyes reminded her of a milky coffee. His nose had a slight bend to it indicating it had been broken. A fine scar traced his left eyebrow.

None of those imperfections detracted from his handsomeness. Even his full lips enticed her to go up on her tiptoe and trace their shape with her tongue.

Lustful thoughts like the ones firing through her neurons this very second had never happened to her before.

"I'm Riley Ashland. I've known Tex for years."

He held out his hand toward her. Instinct had her reaching for it. Warmth zinged through her at the contact. Maria found it almost impossible to release her hold on his flesh. But she managed it, only to regret the loss of warmth moments later.

"Maria Moretti. I've only known Mel and Tex for a couple of years."

Wow, I haven't lost the ability to speak.

For a few seconds she wondered if she would have the ability to speak at all.

"How about we all go into the living room?" Tex suggested, amusement lacing his words.

Oh no. No. No. No. Tex and Melody weren't setting her up were they? This wasn't some sort of blind date arrangement.

She stalled Tex's progress with a hand on his arm. Once she saw Riley had entered the living room, she turned to face her friend's husband. "You're not setting me up, are you?"

Tex laughed at her suggestion. "No. Trust me, I

know better than to try and get you to do something you don't want to do. Ash, turned up unexpectedly."

"Ash?"

"Yeah, Riley," Tex chuckled. "His nickname is *Ash*. Like mine is Tex."

"Right. Okay. Well you and Mel better not be up to something. I came here to decompress not to have to worry about some sort of matchmaking scheme."

Tex gripped her shoulders. "You can relax here. I've already said you're safe. But know this: Mel and I worry about you. I can tell by looking at you that something is wrong. Something is weighing you down. It's up to you if you share it with us. I hope you do, though."

Tex's words should alleviate her concerns, and they had when she'd arrived. Now there was another person in the house. A person she didn't know anything about. "And what about this Riley or *Ash* dude, is he trustworthy?"

"He's an ex-SEAL. I trust him with my life, Mel's life and my girl's life."

Maria nodded. "Okay. I guess we'd better not leave him hanging out alone."

Straightening her shoulders, she walked away from Tex and into the living room. Riley had made himself comfortable on the couch and was reading something on his phone. He looked up and smiled, his eyes crinkling in the corners. It brightened his whole face.

Shit. That smile was a lethal weapon.

For endless seconds they appraised each other, her standing in the doorway, Riley lounging on the couch.

She jumped when a hand landed on her shoulder. A quick look over her shoulder revealed Tex standing beside her.

"Don't sneak up on me like that?"

"Sorry. I wanted to let you know that Mel will be here in a few she's just changing Hope. I've got to go meet the school bus."

"No worries, Tex. We've got this." Riley spoke up. "I'll look after your guest."

A raised eyebrow from Tex had Maria switching her gaze to the other man in the room. His expression gave nothing away. Somehow though, Maria, had an idea that a silent military type conversation had passed between the two of them.

She rolled her eyes and sat down in a chair opposite to where Riley sat, his gaze assessing.

God save her from alpha men. She dealt with plenty of them at the hospital. Not to mention her residency class. She was a damn good surgeon and some of the guys in her class didn't appreciate her skill. Their actions toward her never bothered her. She didn't let it.

"Tex tells me you're an ex-SEAL. How long have you been out of the military?"

"Five years. I was in for a total of twelve."

His easy answer surprised her. For some reason she expected him to not be so forthcoming with information about his time in the service. Although she hadn't asked him a question directly related to what he'd done.

Why had he left though? She couldn't see any physical injury to him, like having lost a limb like Tex.

"What made you decide to leave your SEAL team?"

"It was time."

A very vague answer, which meant there was way more to the story than he was telling her. Considering they'd met only ten minutes ago his reluctance to bare his soul to her was understandable. But with this guy here, the last thing she wanted to do was talk to Mel and Tex about the reason for her trip.

"What do you do for work now?" she asked.

"A little bit of this. A little bit of that."

Another non-committal reply, warning bells rang in her head. Who was this guy? Tex said he trusted him, but even the most loyal, patriotic person could be swayed to take some money and work for her father. It was how he'd managed to stay out of jail. Police and judges were all on his payroll.

Maria stood abruptly. She needed to get out of there. Tex assured her she would be safe, now with this unexpected guest, she wasn't too sure.

She'd almost made her escape when Melody walked into the room.

"Whoa, Maria, where are you running off too? I haven't gotten a chance to talk to you."

Maria was immediately engulfed in a hug from Melody. This was one person she knew she could trust. After having someone stalk her and maim her dog, Melody wouldn't be entrapped by her family.

As much as she'd wanted to get out of dodge, she needed to unburden herself.

"I was going to see where you were."

"I think I scared her."

Maria pulled herself out of Melody's embrace and whipped around to look at Riley, jamming her hands on her hips. "Excuse me, that couldn't be further from the truth. I've had to deal with far scarier surgeons and registrars than you."

The arrogant bastard smiled at her. Smiled like he knew exactly what had been going through her mind. It didn't help that his smile only highlighted his handsomeness.

"That may be. But you don't trust me and if

Melody hadn't walked in, you'd have been out that front door quicker than a jack rabbit."

How she hated arrogant men who thought they knew exactly what was going through her mind. The fact that this time he was right, grated on her every nerve.

"Okay, you two, back to your corners." Melody interrupted the silent war waging between them.

Maria kept glaring at Riley, ignoring Melody's instructions. Riley raised an eyebrow before breaking their connection, and going back to where he'd been sitting before Melody had joined them.

She had no intention of sitting down yet, not until she felt comfortable around him. Which she didn't see happening anytime soon.

"How well do you know, Riley?" Maria had never beaten around the bush before. She had no plans to start now.

"A couple of years. He and Tex weren't on the same SEAL team, but they knew of each other. Tex has had him investig—" Melody shut her mouth quickly. Her eyes widened in a *oh-shit-I've-said-too-much*.

Maria looked between Melody and Riley. He'd put his neutral expression back on his face again.

What the hell was going on here?

Why exactly is Riley Ashland here?

Enough was enough. Tex had been evasive when he'd said Riley was passing through. It was becoming clearer and clearer it was no co-incidence Riley happened to be at Tex and Melody's house the same time as she was.

"You need to be straight with me, Melody. What are you and Tex up to? And please don't try and put me off with an *oh he's just passing through* line. It won't fly with me."

Melody sighed. "Fine. When I called I knew something was wrong the moment you started talking. I don't know what it is, but I know you wouldn't have asked to come up here if it wasn't something big. Tex agreed with me. He phoned Riley and asked him if he could come here, too."

Maria didn't know what to think. In her life, she'd never had anyone look out for her the way Tex and Melody were doing right now.

With a glance over her shoulder, she noted Riley had stood and was watching her, assessing her every action.

"Is he here to act as a bodyguard? Because if that's what you're all thinking I need then you can forget it. I don't need a bodyguard."

A hand landed on her shoulder. Her skin tingled and fire meandered through her blood. She knew who was touching her.

Riley.

This feeling coursing through her was more dangerous than having a gun held to her head. In a situation like that, the outcome was predictable—dead or alive. But with these sensations, anything could happen and she wasn't prepared to let herself succumb to them.

She shook his hand away and turned to face him. "Look, I don't know what they've told you. But I'm fine. I was stressed when I spoke to Melody. Nothing is wrong."

"Really." Only a person from the south could draw out the word like that.

Tex.

It probably wasn't wise to turn her back to Riley, but she had no choice. The only time she never looked someone in the eye when she spoke to them was when she was performing surgery.

Turning back she glared at Tex. "Yes, really."

"So you didn't perform a surgical procedure in a non-medical facility the other night and the Feds didn't visit you the day after performing said surgery."

With his arms crossed over his wide chest, Tex looked every inch the former SEAL he'd been.

Formidable.

Large.

Threatening, but also protective at the same time.

Lying to him wouldn't be the smartest thing to do. Plus she'd come to see her friends because she needed to talk about what had happened to her. It didn't mean she needed a bodyguard, though. She knew how to look after herself. That was one thing her father had taught her.

"Fine. Yes, everything you say is true. I performed surgery on my Uncle Vittorio, my father's right hand man. Yes, the Feds visited me asking me about the event. And yes, I am the daughter of mob boss Giovanni Moretti." Her chest rising up and down rapidly from her outburst, she looked around the room. "Is everyone happy now?"

"We're only just beginning, Doc."

Maria didn't like the sound of that. And she especially didn't like the sound of it coming from Riley. And where did he get off giving her a nickname?

Perhaps coming to Melody had been a bad idea. Had she jumped from the frying pan head long into a cauldron of fire?

She was reminded of those words the next afternoon when she walked to the back patio and found Riley already sitting out there playing with Baby.

All damn day Riley was there whenever she turned around or walked into a room.

"My God, can you not give me some space?"

She'd specifically come outside because it was the one place she figured he wouldn't be, but there he was, eyes hidden by sunglasses, hair ruffled in that sexy morning after look that begged for her to run her fingers through it.

Shit.

This had to stop and it had stop now. She couldn't afford to let herself entertain any thoughts of getting to know Riley any better. They may not have said anything to her but she wasn't dumb. The only reason he was sitting on Tex's back porch was because Tex had decided that she needed a bodyguard.

Nope not happening.

"There's a whole back yard, I'm sure you can find some space to do whatever it is you wanted to do."

"What I wanted to do was get away from *you.*" She crossed her arms over her chest. "How have you been everywhere I've been today? Geez, even before knowing where I'm going you're somehow there."

Maria bit down on her temper as he shrugged his broad shoulders while smiling as though he had not one care in the world.

"Just lucky I guess."

"Well, if it wouldn't be too much trouble, can you

go find someone else to bother? I'm sure Tex would love to talk to you."

Riley stood and bent to pick up the stick he'd been teasing Baby with, his shorts hugged his ass tightly. As a doctor she'd seen her fair share of bodies, but Riley's was prime A grade quality. It was clear as the nose on her face, even though he'd left the military, he hadn't given up on the strict physical regime they put their bodies through to keep themselves in peak physical condition to handle any situation while they were in the service.

As he walked over to her, twirling the stick in his hand, Maria tamped down the urge to step back. He got within a foot of her and stopped.

"Here, you play with Baby." He tossed the stick to her and she caught it without thinking about it. "I'll leave you to it."

"Good idea. Make sure you keep that up for the rest of the weekend."

"I'll think about it," he whispered into her ear.

A heady mix of his cologne and unique masculine smell assailed her senses as he walked back into the house, tempting her to follow him. The man should come with a warning—*stay away at all costs*.

Thank goodness she only had one more day to get through and then she'd never have to see Riley Ashland again.

CHAPTER FOUR

Watching from the shadows, Riley observed Maria as she stopped, phone in hand, after exiting the elevator to the basement parking lot of the hospital. He'd been watching her from afar for over a week now.

As Tex had predicted, Maria refused to have Riley act as her bodyguard. After her admission of the surgery she'd performed on her uncle, he'd given Tex a look that said *back off*.

Later that night he and Tex had decided that regardless of what Maria said Riley was going to protect her. He knew it would be impossible to follow her every move while she worked. He had no plans to sit in and watch while she performed surgery. He'd seen enough maimed bodies while he'd been in the military.

Also he'd worked hard with counseling to deal with lingering PTSD issues upon his return to the States and his acclimatization back into society. He knew if he saw any of her surgeries it would most likely trigger an attack.

Even though he wasn't physically watching her in the hospital, Tex had hacked into the hospital's security systems that enabled him to keep an eye on her through an app on his IPad. He usually had Tex monitoring Maria when she was in surgery. During those times Riley was able to work on some of the other cases they had at the office.

The workload was light with the impending birth of Lily and Storm's child. Riley knew the other man didn't want to be caught out on a job when Lily went into labor. This job for Tex had come at the right time.

The revving of a car engine drew his attention. It appeared to be coming from the level up. His senses were on alert as Maria headed toward where her car was parked. Riley matched her steps. The tires on the car squealed as it made its progress through the lot. Not an unusual occurrence, but the high-pitched wail of it suggested the car was doing more than the suggested speed limit. Picking up his pace, he dodged between the parked cars to get closer to Maria. She walked into the middle of the driveway when the car pealed around the corner.

The bright headlights illuminated the surprise on Maria's face. He was five feet away from her. The car looked like it was slowing down, but he couldn't be too sure.

"Fuck." He sprinted out and wrapped an arm around Maria, twisting so he hit the concrete first and cushioned Maria's fall. The car screeched to a halt. Riley attempted to position himself so he could see the license plate, but the fall had winded him and all he could do was lie on the cold ground clutching Maria tightly, gasping for air as the car engine revved up and sped away.

Riley didn't think the car would come back and try again, but he wasn't planning on taking any chances.

"We need to move," he wheezed the words out in between attempts to gain back his breath. An elbow to his gut wasn't helping his shortness of breath.

"What the hell was that for?" Maria scrambled to her feet. He missed the warmth of her body against his.

"You save a girl's life and this is the thanks you get." Riley muttered, grimacing as he stood.

"I didn't need rescuing, thank you very much."

The last thing he wanted to do was argue with her, but that's all she seemed to enjoy doing. He grabbed her hand and walked to where they couldn't be seen by anyone or any cars.

"I'm not sure if you're aware, but that car wasn't just a driver speeding through the parking garage in a hurry to get home. Whoever was behind that wheel was coming for you."

It shouldn't, but satisfaction filled him when he saw the color drain from her face. He had contacts on the streets. Ones who'd helped him with his PI cases before and after he'd joined forces with Storm. From his investigations, word on the ground was Giovanni wanted his daughter back in the fold, even though he promised her she could have her own life. And Giovanni had promised a big payout for whoever could get his daughter back to him.

Riley was pretty sure Maria hoped she was fully free from her father, but deep down she probably knew she never would be.

"How do you know they were after me?"

"Doc, I've been here for the last fifteen minutes. No one walked out before you did."

"Maybe they came out before you arrived and was on the phone. There could be any number of reasons why that car was in hurry. Going after me couldn't be one of them."

"Maria, come on, you don't really believe that do you?" He injected enough incredulousness in his tone to get his point across.

"Whatever. Now can you please let me go so I can go to my car and go home."

The fact Maria hadn't questioned him as to why he was in the parking garage told him what she wasn't telling him. She was more shaken up than she wanted to admit.

"You're in no state to drive. I'll drive you home."

The argument he expected to get from her at his declaration didn't arrive. He wasn't going to push his luck, so he steered her to where he'd parked his car.

Once he got her settled in he surveyed the area around him. A group of people were walking out of the elevator lobby, all of them chatting amongst themselves so he didn't see them as a threat. There was no echo of a car revving its engine to concern him.

He got into his car when his phone vibrated pulling it out of his pocket he saw he had an incoming text message from Tex.

I SAW WHAT HAPPENED. ARE YOU AND MARIA OKAY?

He quickly typed a response.

WE'RE FINE. I DIDN'T GET A GOOD LOOK AT THE LICENSE PLATE BUT IT'S SAFE TO SAY THE VEHICLE WAS TARGETING MARIA. I'M DRIVING HER HOME NOW.

He started the car and before pulling out another message came through.

Good idea. Talk soon.

Riley tossed his phone into the center console and pulled out of the parking bay. He looked over to Maria and found her gazing out the window. He couldn't work out if the slump in her shoulders was from the shock of what happened or if she was tired from working a twelve-hour shift.

Once they were safely out of the parking garage and Riley had made a few random turns to make sure they weren't being followed he allowed himself to relax a bit.

"Tough day at work?"

"Why were you in the parking garage tonight?"

Ah, the haze of shock was beginning to lift.

"Would you believe me if I said happy coincidence?"

"Oh shit. No. Please don't tell me you ignored what I said the weekend we were at Tex's place and you're playing bodyguard to me."

He knew she was a smart woman.

"I could deny it, but I won't."

"Ha, you already tried to deny it, *Ash*. I swear when I get home I'm going to phone Tex and give him hell for thinking he could do this to me."

"Before you do that, perhaps you'd like to think

about what would've happened if I hadn't been there tonight."

"Well, we won't know now will we."

This was a conversation he didn't want to have while driving the streets of Brooklyn. He pulled into a convenience store's parking lot.

"Why are we stopping?" Maria asked. "I didn't say I was thirsty or hungry. I want to go home."

Riley swiveled in his seat so he could look at her. "Let's get back to what we were discussing. You know full well that if I hadn't been there, you'd either be seriously injured, or lying on a cold metal slab in the morgue, or being transported again to some other destination, and this time maybe not to perform surgery."

"You don't know that."

"It's conceivable that it may not be him, but someone else who could be after you. You're the only daughter of one of the biggest mobsters in New York. I'd say getting hold of you would appeal to many families."

He let the words sink in. The time for being gentle was over. Tonight had been a blatant attempt to harm her. No way was Riley going to let that happen. He hadn't lost anyone on his watch since he started his business. He wasn't planning to begin now.

"I know who my father is, but he promised he wouldn't hurt me."

"And he's a man of his word is he?"

Maria opened her mouth and closed it just as quickly, her body sagging in the leather seat. His point had been made.

He put the car back in gear and exited the parking lot. Riley knew once they got to his place the arguments would start again. Initially he'd been planning on taking her to her place. The possibility that her apartment was being watched was pretty high. It was the first thing that should've entered his mind when they got into the car. Only his focus then had been on getting her out of there without the other car returning.

When they pulled into the underground garage of his apartment complex, out of the corner of his eye he caught Maria straightening in her seat.

"This *is not* my place."

"No, we're at mine." Riley pulled into his designated space and turned the engine off. "And don't even try and argue with me. Until I can check it out, you're not returning to your apartment. It could be being watched. You're safe here."

"Oh my God, aren't you taking this all out of proportion? We don't even know if what happened at work was an attempt to harm me or a simple case of a car driving too fast."

Frustration welled inside him. "Haven't we already determined that what happened to you wasn't a simple case of a random accident? Jesus, Maria, you may not want to hear it. You may not even like it. But someone is after you. Now, we're going to get out of the car and go up to my place."

"You don't have to speak to me like I'm five."

"Then don't act like you are. You're a surgeon. You're the daughter of a high profile mobster. You performed surgery that wasn't conducted at or sanctioned by a hospital. From that moment on your life took a u-turn. It's time to face facts you need protection. Whether you like it or not—I'm your man."

He got out of the car and walked around to her door, he opened it and looked down at her still sitting in the leather chair, her seatbelt firmly dissecting her breasts.

"What's it going to be?" he asked.

"Do I have a choice?"

Riley leaned into the car until his lips were millimeters away from her ear. "No."

He breathed in. Beneath the aroma of antiseptic associated with hospitals, he could make out a hint of something floral. It teased his senses, making him want to see if he could find further traces of it on her body.

Maria Moretti was becoming a temptation he hadn't known he wanted.

CHAPTER FIVE

Why had she been born a Moretti?

The question scrolled through her mind like the banner at the bottom of a television screen blasting that latest news headlines.

It wasn't the first time she'd asked herself that question. Although, ever since she started her surgical residency, it hadn't been a frequent mind visitor. Naively, she'd thought because her father hadn't attempted to contact her, he was finally granting her wish of letting her be Maria Moretti the surgeon, not Maria Moretti only daughter of Giovanni Moretti. An independent woman forging her own path in the world without the specter of her father and his business trailing behind her.

She'd been a fool. How could she have ever thought her father would let her be free of him? Of course, for him, having a surgeon on the payroll would be very handy. Someone who could take care of any medical emergencies without having to alert a hospital or the cops.

Now here she stood in an apartment of a man she'd met twice who was now her bodyguard.

Great. Seriously it was fantastic how quickly her life had gone to shit.

"Can I get you something to drink?"

Maria steeled her spine against the shiver threatening to slither down her spine. Her senses had been on high alert ever since he'd leaned down in the car and whispered in her ear.

One word.

One friggin word was all he said, but the way she'd practically melted into his car seat like ice cream on a hot summer's day, he may as well have recited a love poem to her.

"Maria? Are you okay?"

A hand waving in front of her face dragged her from the revere she'd fallen into. "I'm fine. And yes, a drink will be good, thank you."

"Wine, coffee, soda, something stronger?"

It would be so nice to ask if he had a smooth bourbon, one that she could shoot down the back of her throat with a flick of her wrist. Unfortunately she had a six o'clock start which meant losing herself in a bottle of alcohol was out of the question.

"I'll take a soda, thanks."

"A soda?" There was no hiding the surprise in Riley's tone.

"Yes, I'm a surgeon. It wouldn't look good if I turn up tomorrow morning with a hangover."

"Fair enough." Riley indicated to a dark brown leather couch. "Take a seat and I'll be right back."

She watched him as he walked away from her. Dressed all in black, he appeared dangerous and lethal. There was no doubt in her mind that he could take down numerous assailants without breaking a sweat.

What was it about ex-Navy SEALs that was so sexy? Was it the allure that they put their lives on the line time after time? Or was it the whole princess needing to be rescued by a prince charging in on his white horse fantasy. Not that she let herself believe she was a princess in a fairytale. Her childhood had showed her first hand that when things go bad, there was no fairy godmother to whisk you to a ball where a handsome prince would save you. She'd saved herself many times, she didn't need anyone else to do it for her. The one person she hadn't been able to save was her mom. Mom always pushed Giovanni. He would never be *Papa* in her mind again. One day she'd come home from school and Mom was nowhere to be seen. The look of menace in her father's eye had her swallowing the questions she wanted to ask.

At the time she'd convinced herself Mom had somehow escaped the wrath and hold of Giovanni Moretti. Now, with the hindsight and maturity of an adult, she knew her mother wasn't living her life in safety. In all likelihood she was resting at the bottom of the Hudson. Or the East river.

Even though her thoughts were miles away, she still looked in the direction of where Riley had retreated. She was in the room, but she wasn't. Her mind had gone to places she normally left locked up tightly. Nothing good came of unlocking those hidden places. The darkness from those memories threatened to suck her into a vortex almost impossible to escape.

"Shit."

It was the last thing she heard before she let herself fall into the vortex. Maybe there it was safer than the world she currently inhabited.

———

Maria had to be dreaming. She was riding the carousel in Central Park, laughing at something the person riding the horse beside her had said.

Up and down they went. Holding hands while their other one gripped the golden pole. Her date's face obscured, pixilated like news documentaries use if they want to keep their interviewee's identity a secret. Then the pixilation was gone and she was standing by a lake, her mystery man cupping her face.

Happiness filled her. A sensation she wasn't used to. Happiness had always been an elusive emotion in her life.

Her man lowered his face toward hers. She lifted hers, eager to look her man in the eye.

Riley. Riley was her dream man.

In slow motion the gap between her lips and his narrowed until they were almost touching.

"Maria. Maria, wake up."

Her eyes snapped open. Reality set in. Her dream forgotten, snatched away before she could know what it felt like to have Riley's lips on hers.

"No." Maria practically shouted the word and pulled away from Riley's hold. She fell back and connected with downy softness. Shaking off the fog of her dream she looked around and found herself lying on a massive bed in a room decorated with pale blue walls and dark mahogany wooden furniture. A room she didn't recognize. She scrambled to a sitting position.

"Hey, take it easy." Gentle hands encouraged her

to lie down again. "You passed out. You don't want to move too quickly."

Laughter bubbled up inside of her. "I passed out? No, I don't think so."

"Trust me, you did. One minute you were standing in the living room, the next you were about to hit the floor. Are you sore anywhere? I know you didn't hit your head when you blacked out because I caught you in time. But in the garage at the hospital, did you hit your head when I pushed you to the ground. Do you remember?"

Oh, she remembered all right. She remembered the glare of headlights heading straight for her. Remembered thinking she needed to move out of the way but couldn't. A familiar face with a menacing grin driving the car. Remembered the feel of strong arms engulfing her, dragging her to the ground—to safety.

Shit. Riley hadn't been lying. Someone had been after her.

"I know who was driving the car."

Riley's fingers tightened around her shoulders before loosening in the next breath. "What? What do you mean?"

"You asked me if I remembered what happened in the garage. It wasn't clear to me straight after it happened. I guess my mind needed to process everything it saw. But just then everything played across my mind and I recalled things I hadn't processed seeing. Like the driver of the car."

A breath hitched in her chest as Riley's large, warm, callused hand cupped her cheek. "Who was it? Who was driving the car?"

"It was my dad's enforcer, Andre. You're right, Riley. I'm not safe. My father wants me back in the fold."

Despair pummeled down on her. The life she'd forged for herself was over. As she'd worked out earlier it had all been an illusion. Her father had given her the impression she was free from his grasp, but she never would be. And she couldn't drag Riley into the mess that was her family.

"I will do everything to keep you safe."

Maria pulled away from Riley's touch. "I think it would be best if you took me home."

"Not happening, Doc."

"Well I can't stay here." She scrambled off the bed and quickly put her hand on the nightstand as a wave of dizziness washed over her.

A hand enclosed around her waist. "You're not going anywhere. Come on, let's sit."

"Not here." She couldn't concentrate in a room with a large bed and a sexy guy. Maria couldn't deny when Riley had wrapped his arm around her, she'd immediately felt protected. Had wanted to lean further into his hold and maybe rest her head on his broad shoulders.

But comforting her wasn't his job. He was here to protect her, even though she'd emphatically told Tex and Riley she didn't need a bodyguard. No way did she plan to be all clichéd and fall in love with her bodyguard.

"Okay, let's go to the kitchen."

He led her out of the room and down the hallway. He lived in a fairly spacious apartment, in a nice building. From the two rooms she'd seen the place had been updated and had a nice modern feel about it. Apartments like this didn't come cheap in New York. Guess there was good money in the protecting people business.

The kitchen he led her into was every woman's dream, if that woman wanted to spend her time cooking and baking up a storm.

Not her. She could cook, not gourmet, but quick easy meals which, with her erratic schedule, were perfect for her.

Riley directed her to a black and chrome stool nestled under the overhang on the kitchen island.

"Take a seat. Now I think I owe you a drink. Your last one ended up on the ground."

Maria hopped up on the stool, propped her elbows on the white, glittery quartz countertop and rested her chin in her hands. "Why did it end up on the ground?"

"Because I couldn't hold the drinks and keep you from falling face first into the floor. I figured the drinks were a better casualty than you."

"Oh." It was all she could muster, as the slow burn of a blush crept up from her neck and over her face. "Umm, thanks for catching me."

"My pleasure," he said as he slid a can of soda across the smooth expanse of the counter toward her.

She grasped the cold can with both hands, fighting to the urge to rub the coolness along her cheeks in an attempt to douse the heat running along her cheekbones.

When Riley sat next to her on another stool, she took a long gulp of her drink. When was the last time a good looking guy had her acting like a teenage girl with a huge crush on the cutest guy in school?

Like, never.

So why was she going to start now? She was a thirty-one year old woman well on her way to becoming an accomplished surgeon.

"I'm guessing from your presence at the hospital that you've been *tailing* me ever since our weekend at Tex's."

"I wouldn't call it tailing. I was doing my job."

"A job I believe I said wasn't necessary."

"Again. Car. Parking garage. Need I say more."

"Fine. But I still think it's wrong that you've been watching me and I didn't know about it."

Riley shrugged, clearly unashamed of his and Tex's underhanded tactics. "That's the whole point. You weren't supposed to know. Our plan was to do surveillance. Understand your daily movements. Watch for interactions that appeared to be every day, but could have ulterior motives. Up until the garage incident Tex and I were beginning to think maybe you were right and your father would leave you alone. However, by you recognizing who was driving the car, only confirmed you aren't safe."

Maria gripped the can, the light aluminum denting beneath her fingertips. "What if my father is having me watched as well? What if he knows you and Tex are helping me? That puts targets on all your backs."

She pushed the stool back, the metal scraping across the tiles, and walked away, heading back down the hallway they'd come down.

Before she'd taken four steps, Riley was beside her, another step he stood in front of her halting her escape.

"Where are you going?"

He'd crossed his arms over his chest again the black long sleeve t-shirt he wore stretched over his bulging biceps. Everything about him screamed protector. She couldn't let herself fall into his safety net.

"I think, for everyone's safety, I should go to my father. Hand myself over to him. I've been fooling myself to ever think I would be free of the Moretti Mob family."

"What do you think that will achicvc?"

"I don't know, but it's got to be better than this."

"What if it isn't? Do you think he's going to welcome you back with open arms?"

"Maybe? I don't know. But at least if I'm with him I won't have to look over my shoulder to see if I'm about to be run over by a car or kidnapped."

"What if he makes you do things you don't want to do? Makes you go against the Hippocratic Oath you took when you became a doctor?"

Frustration boiled over to anger inside of her and she pushed against his chest. It was like hitting a brick wall. Riley didn't even flinch. "Get out of my way."

The next instant she was engulfed in strong arms and her face was buried against Riley's hard chest. The fight drained out of her and was replaced by tears. She never cried. Tonight, in Riley's arms she allowed herself to cry.

"Shhh, Doc. We'll work this out."

"I just want to be free." She mumbled the words against his chest.

"I know you do."

Maria pulled away and looked up at Riley. He was staring down at her. His brown eyes radiated warmth and she wanted to sink into them. Her gaze trailed down over his lips. Their fullness tempted her to taste them.

Would it be so wrong to seek comfort when her life was in such turmoil? Not giving herself a chance to think through how bad an idea it was she rose up on tiptoe and placed her lips against Riley's.

A quick touch and then she'd disengage herself from his hold and get him to take her to father's house. At least she would have this memory to hang onto when things got terrible, as she was sure they would with her father.

As she went to pull away from him, Riley tugged her tighter, changed his stance and deepened the kiss, taking full control of it.

Maria sighed and gave herself over to his embrace. If this was what being cherished felt like, she wanted a lifetime of it. Even if it was with her bodyguard. The one person she'd sworn she would stay away from.

CHAPTER SIX

*S*top. *Pull away.*

The words resounded in his mind, but his body refused to co-operate. Kissing Maria was entirely the wrong thing to do. He never kissed clients. He'd protected plenty of beautiful women, some who hadn't been too shy to let him know they wouldn't mind some extra benefits. He let them down gently and went on his way never giving them another thought. But the vulnerability in Maria's eyes drew him in.

The way she'd stood there and looked him in the eye telling him she would go back to her father's place. Give in to the man she was trying to breakaway from.

No way would he let that happen.

Nor could he let the kiss go on for much longer. If

it did he would let a certain part of his anatomy take control. The problem was, Maria fit in his arms like no other women ever had.

He was in trouble.

Deep, deep trouble.

With his body screaming *no*, but his mind yelling *yes*, he loosened his hold on Maria and took a step back.

"I'm sorry," his words came out croaky so he cleared his throat. "Kissing probably wasn't a good idea."

The sleepy, languid look in Maria's eyes disappeared. He mourned the loss. The looseness their kiss had given her limbs drained out and her muscles tensed beneath the scrubs she wore.

Riley immediately regretted his words. Sure it was a bad idea, but he didn't have to say it out loud. He'd enjoyed every single second of having Maria in his arms. In other circumstances he might have taken it further. He could've, right now, been kissing his way down her body. Learning the areas that made her sigh, and areas that made her cry out in ecstasy.

His already hard flesh hardened even further with his x-rated thoughts.

"Can you take me to my father's now?"

"No."

"What do you mean no? You can't keep me here if

I don't want to be. It's my life to ruin any way I chose."

Against his better judgment, his fingers curled over her shoulders. He couldn't seem to stop touching her.

"You're not going anywhere, Maria. I'm not going to let you sacrifice yourself. Tex and I will come up with a solution to this problem. Until we do, I think it would be best if you stayed here. Your place isn't safe anymore."

Having her stay in his apartment was going to test his resolve. But there was no way he was going to let her go back to her own place. The potential of her being harmed was too high.

"Look, I know you and Tex were both SEALs, dealing with my father is completely different to the situations you've had to deal with. Whatever it is you do for a living now, it won't help in breaking me free from my father's clutches."

If only Maria knew the shit he'd seen and the crap he'd dealt with in the past. Riley knew extracting her from the Mob was going to be an uphill battle. He had no idea how he would manage it, but somehow, he'd get her free so she could follow her dreams.

"You'd be surprised at some of the stuff I've had to do. Not just when I was deployed, but when I was stateside as well. There's a lot of bad shit in the world, Doc. I've seen plenty and I've rescued people who thought they had no escape."

Before she could answer his doorbell rang. Immediately he went on alert. It was getting late and he hadn't invited anyone over to his place. How had the person got past the night doorman?

Unless the person knocking on his door was on his list of approved visitors. Still he wasn't taking any chances.

"Go into my bedroom and don't make a sound," he instructed Maria. He reached down and pulled the gun from his ankle holster. He looked to see if she had followed his instructions but Maria was rooted to the spot, her eyes fixed on his Glock. "I said go."

"Wouldn't it be safer if I come with you to the door?"

"No. Now don't argue." He canted his head toward his bedroom, relief pouring through him when she started moving. For a moment there he thought he'd have to hoist her over his shoulder and take her to his room.

The doorbell rang again. This time the person pressed the buzzer longer than was strictly polite.

With all the stealth he'd learned in his training, Riley stalked to the front door. Gun raised in the ready he looked through the peephole. When he saw who was standing on the opposite side to his closed door, his shoulders released the tension that had been riding them and lowered his gun.

Unlocking the door, he pulled it open. "What the fuck, Robot? What are you doing here?"

His former SEAL team mate smiled at him, his gaze taking in the gun still at Riley's side. "Hell of a welcome."

Riley laughed, before bending and putting his gun back in the holster. He straightened and held the door wide open for Robot. "You can never be too careful these days. Come on in." Robot stepped into his hallway. Riley clasped his out stretched hand and they did the whole slap-on-the-back man hug.

"Nice digs you've got here, Ash. Certainly beats where I've been the last month."

They walked down the hallway toward his living room. Riley still surprised at seeing his friend in his apartment. It couldn't have been a coincidence that Robot showed up on his doorstep after he spoke to Tex about getting in touch with him when the team got back stateside.

"I take it Tex spoke to you?" Riley asked.

"Affirmative."

Riley wasn't sure what to make of Robot being here. They hadn't spoken or emailed in over a year. He knew the team had been deployed for six months, but once their tour was over they'd remained in the

US. But that didn't mean they remained in there. No doubt they were called out to covert missions that no one knew about.

"Can I get you something to drink?" Riley asked.

"I take it I'm not in any danger? Or do you like to invite the enemy into your house and offer them drinks."

Riley turned and saw Maria standing in the doorway. "Did I say it was safe to come out?"

"Well, no because it looked like you were busy with your bromance and forgot about me."

Robot busted out laughing. "She's feisty this one."

Riley shook his head. He'd been so shocked to find him standing on the other side of the door that he had forgotten about Maria hiding out in his bedroom. He walked over to where she stood and reached out to touch her arm. Immediately the air sizzled around them at the contact.

"Maria, I'd like you to meet Robot. He was on my SEAL team."

"Robot?" Maria went over to shake his hand. "You poor thing."

"It's okay, Robot is his nickname." He looked over to where Robot stood, gave him a look and when Robot nodded he continued. "His full name is Brendan Dean."

"Good to meet you, Maria." Robot stood and clasped Maria's hand.

"Likewise. Which name do you prefer?"

"I'll answer to both."

Riley narrowed his eyes as he watched the interaction, wanting to see if Maria reacted to Robot's touch like she did to his. He immediately shook the thought off. He wasn't jealous. So what if they'd shared a hot kiss earlier. He'd already told himself he wasn't going to get involved with Maria. His track record with women wasn't the best and his job wasn't conducive to long term relationships.

The one and only serious relationship he'd ever had, had ended during his first deployment. Nothing like receiving a *Dear John* letter or in this case email when you're about to embark on a serious mission. Thank goodness Storm had been there to pull him back from stepping on a landmine that would've taken them both out.

He disappeared out of the room to get drinks for everyone and took the time to get his thoughts away from the past and firmly on the issue at hand— protecting Maria and finding a way to grant her the freedom she badly wanted.

When he walked back into the room Maria and Robot were laughing. Both of them looked up as he slammed the bottles on the table a little harder than he thought.

"What are you to laughing about?"

"Oh. Robot, here was telling me about how he got his nickname. I told him I wanted to see a demo of his robot dance."

"I told her my dancing days were over," he said as he reached for one of the beers on the table.

Maria picked up the can of soda he'd also bought in and looked up at him. "I heard Tex call you Ash while we were at his house. I guess that's just a shortened version of your last name."

"Pretty much."

Maria studied him as she took a sip of her drink. "Are you disappointed you didn't get your nickname in a unique way?"

"No. I was fine with Ash. Now how about we leave talk of nicknames and return to the task at hand?"

Marie pouted and he bit back the urge to lean forward and suck her protruding bottom lip into his mouth. Fortunately the pout quickly disappeared. "I've told you what I want to do, Riley. I want to go back to my father's house."

"And I've told you that's not an option."

"I refuse to spend the rest of my life looking over my shoulder. Wondering when he'll strike again. At least if I'm living under his roof I won't have to do that."

"And living under his roof might lead to your death."

Her face blanched at the starkness of his words. He hadn't sugar coated what he'd told her before. He wasn't planning to start now.

"I'm his only child. I doubt my father really wants me to die."

"So what do you call tonight then? You recognized Andre behind the wheel of the car. I don't believe what happened tonight was an accident. I think it was a warning."

"Ash is right, Maria," Robot interjected. "It would serve you no good to go to your father's place."

"And how much do you know about this, Mr. Robot? You just walked in here."

"Okay, let's all take a breath," Riley said. "Fighting isn't going to help us come up with a good plan. Maria, I'm pretty sure Tex would've given Robot a basic rundown of what's happened."

"Did you tell Tex what happened?" she asked.

Riley shrugged. "I didn't have to. He knew."

"How?"

"It's never wise to question how Tex has knowledge of these things. The less you know the better it is for you. But he's been hacking into the hospital's security cameras all week to watch you. I'm guessing he was doing the same thing tonight."

Riley knew she wasn't going to like hearing what he'd just said, but she had to know all that he and Tex had done this week.

"I thought it was just you watching me."

"No, it was the both of us. I can't follow you around the hospital can I? I'm sure you go into restricted areas. Plus I don't really want to watch you perform surgeries. With Tex's computer skills it made sense for him to do what he did. Trust me when I say, Tex's ability to access security cameras around the place has saved more than one person."

"Maria, I know I only met you a half hour ago, but you have to trust what Ash and Tex are saying and doing. Plus now that the team is stateside, we'll be more than happy to provide support where we can. I'll talk to the Commander and clear it with him should the need for action arise."

"I don't believe this." Maria covered her face with her hands. "I can't let you do this. I can't let you all put yourselves in danger, just to save me."

Riley looked over at Robot, he never expected their help, but he couldn't deny having the guys at his back should he need them was a welcome thought.

He squatted down in front of Maria, pulling her hands away from her face. He held them tightly, waiting until she looked at him. "Doc, they're SEALs, danger is their middle name. Besides I don't imagine things are going to get to the stage where we have to call in the big guns. But knowing I have my former team at my back if I need them is a big help."

"I hardly think the US Military wants to get involved with the mafia," Maria commented drily. "If you think they're going to be useful then fine, but I'm not happy with all of this."

Riley couldn't help but agree with her comments. Anything the team did would have to be on the down low and on their free time. But as Robot said, their Commander was a good guy he'd clear them to help out where they can, especially if a woman was involved. Commander Black had lost his niece when she'd been kidnapped and killed by her biological father. If he asked the Commander if the team could assist with keeping Maria safe, Riley had no doubt his former leader would allow the team to do whatever was needed to help.

"I think I should leave." Robot stood. "Ash, if you need us you have my email. But also let Tex know he can get in touch with us if you can't."

"Thanks, I appreciate it, man." Riley fixed his gaze on Maria. "Don't move. I'm going to see Robot out then we can talk some more and eat."

"As if I could leave. For all I know the doorman is

probably an ex-SEAL or some other ex-special forces guy which makes leaving virtually impossible."

"Surprisingly, he's not." He leaned forward and kissed her forehead, before following Robot out of the room. He lowered his voice as they reached the door. "Why don't you speak to Italy and see if he can find out anything about Moretti. I know from my contacts that he wants his daughter back, but the reason as to why they can't find out. Plus what happened tonight was definitely an attempt on her life. I don't know if this Andre guy took it too far or he had orders to eliminate her."

"Will do. Italy's got family everywhere. I'm sure he'll be able to find something out."

Riley clapped Robot on the shoulder. "Thanks for coming tonight. I really appreciate it. And I'm sorry for—"

"Say no more," Robot interrupted. "Once a team member always a team member, you know that. I know if I needed help, you'd be there no questions asked.

Riley nodded. Nothing more needed to be said. "Take care."

Robot walked out before stopping and turning to look at him again. "By the way say hi to Storm for me. How are he and Lily?"

"They're fine. Lily is about to have her baby so

Storm's a bit tense. But apart from that, Lily's lingerie business is as busy as ever."

"Good to hear. I'll be in touch."

Riley closed the door, pausing for a moment before heading back to the living room and Maria, a woman who was going to keep him on his toes. He wasn't ashamed to admit he didn't mind it. How could anyone not admire Maria? Her strength of character and determination to keep everyone around her safe appealed to him. More than it should. But he couldn't let it. His focus had to be on protecting Maria and not repeating their kiss from earlier, no matter how tempted he was.

CHAPTER SEVEN

W as it mandatory for all SEALs to be over six feet, built like a brick shed and so good looking that they could be on the cover of a men's magazine? Even though Robot was good looking with his piercing blue eyes, broad shoulders and closely cropped dirty blonde hair. He didn't make her heart race like one look from Riley '*Ash*' Ashland did. Nor did Robot make her want to throw every rule she had about not getting involved in a relationship until she was done with her residency out the window.

Relationship.

What the hell was she thinking? Her life was in danger and here she is thinking about investigating the possibility of a relationship between her and

Riley. Maybe she had hit her head when she'd passed out.

"I ordered some Chinese for dinner."

"That's fine."

Food was the last thing on her mind. She kept her back to him, knowing if she turned she'd be tempted to walk over to him and ask him to hug her again. Not the smartest thing to do.

"Are you okay, Doc?" He asked the question so quietly she was surprised she'd heard it.

Doc. No one has ever given me a nickname. Why did he have to be my first?

She gave up keeping her distance and turned around. He stood a foot away from her. Concern darkened his eyes until they looked almost black.

"Do you really think it's possible I can breakaway from my father's hold?"

Maria held her breath as Riley closed the distance between them. She fought the urge to let her head fall forward onto his chest. As it was, when his fingers brushed her cheek to hook a lock of hair behind her ears she swayed toward him.

It had to be the intense situation she found herself in for her to be this needy around a man. But she was tired as well. So tired of having to worry about her father and the consequences his lifestyle could rain down on her.

"Anything's possible, Doc. I'll do whatever I can to ensure you have a life free from your father's hold."

How she wanted to believe him. She really did. But this was the Mob they were talking about. After her mother's disappearance, she'd held herself back from getting close to anyone because she'd been scared her father would make the next person she cared about disappear. She'd alienated herself from the friends she'd made in school and had concentrated on her studies. The same when she'd been gone to college. Not only were her studies intense and required her whole focus, her relationships had been kept to a minimum. She'd go on the occasional date and if she liked them she'd sleep with them, but she never let them get close. It was safer that way.

The sound of a phone ringing jarred her and she took a step away from Riley.

"That will be the food. I'll be right back. If you want to freshen up, there's a bathroom right there." He pointed to a closed just to the right of the entrance to the living room.

While he dealt with the food, Maria washed her hands, grimacing at the sight of herself in the mirror. The dark circles under her eyes were more pronounced against the paleness of her face. Her hair was a flyaway mess and she had a smudge of dirt on her cheek.

How the heck had Riley wanted to kiss her when she looked liked this? She splashed water on her face, washing away the dirt. She smoothed her damp hands over her hair. There was nothing she could do about her clothes. She'd lived in scrubs for the last five or so years of her life.

She had nothing to wear. She couldn't stay here.

Maria burst out of the hallway bathroom and strode into the living room. "You have to take me back to my place."

Riley looked up from where he'd been putting their meal out on the dark wooden coffee table. "We've already been over this more times that I like. You're not going back to your apartment. It's not safe."

"But I have to work in the morning. I need underwear. A pair of clean scrubs."

"Sit and eat. I'll get someone to go to your place and pack for you."

"I will not sit down. And I don't want some stranger going through my apartment, not to mention my clothes. If it's not safe for me to go there, how can it be safe for someone else too?"

"You need to start trusting me, Maria, because I'm not going to argue with you over every little thing."

"But."

"No. Enough. Now eat."

As if to emphasize his point, Riley grabbed one of the white square cardboard containers and a set of chopsticks and started to eat.

The aroma of the food wafted to her and her stomach grumbled in appreciation. It had been a long time since she'd eaten and it was well after nine in the evening.

"Fine."

A soft knock on the door penetrated the blissful sleep Maria was having. She rolled over and stuck her head under the pillow. She didn't remember her bed feeling this soft.

Another knock and then the door opened a crack.

Who the hell was coming into her room?

"Doc."

The whispered word had her bolting upright in bed. Everything from the night before came flashing back to her.

The car.

Riley.

Passing out.

Riley.

Chinese food.

Kissing Riley.

Her life in a mess.

Kissing Riley.

"What?" she grumbled.

"I take it you're not a morning person?"

Maria sighed, normally waking up wasn't an issue. She loved the anticipation of a new day and what surgeries she might be assisting with or performing herself. Of course, that was before her life hit the shit pile.

"It's okay, Riley. Come in."

Her frustrations disappeared when she spied the red coffee mug in his hand. He reached her bedside and placed the mug on the nightstand. She reached out and grabbed it, inhaling deeply.

"The elixir of Gods," she murmured as she took her first sip of the hot liquid. The richness of Brazilian coffee beans coated her tongue. "Damn, this is good coffee."

Riley chuckled. "Glad something meets your approval. I've got your clothes here." He slung a bag off his shoulder.

Maria knew better than to question how he'd done it. "Thanks."

"It's five now, you need to be at work at six thirty, right?"

She took another drink of her coffee. At this

moment she didn't want to go anywhere. She wanted to savor this magnificent beverage.

"I can put more in a travel mug for you?"

"It's that obvious is it?" she said laughing.

"Kind of." Riley joined in her laughter and she thought he was going to sit on the bed next to her, but he stopped.

"In comparison to the coffee at the hospital, this is black gold."

"Why don't you get yourself ready and I'll fix you that travel mug. We'll need to leave soon so we get you to work on time."

Nerves bubbled in her belly at the thought of walking into the hospital. Would she be putting her colleagues in danger as well?

"Whatever you're thinking, stop it. Everything will be fine. It will be just like it's been for the last week, only today I'll drop you at the door and then Tex will take over like he's done every day. What I'll need you to do is text me when you're finished for the day. If you want, I can meet you for lunch as well."

"What will you do while I'm working?"

"The less you know the better. Now, you'd better get moving."

He walked out of the room before she had a chance to question him further about what he was going to be doing. Hopefully he would be looking at ways to get her away from her father. Maybe she should call her father herself? Talk to him and reason with him.

Of course, there was also the Feds and their investigation into her operating on her uncle. It was a mess. A tangled web that whenever she tried to extract herself from it the silky, sticky threads clung to her, trapping her deeper and deeper until escape was impossible.

Stop it.

Never before had she let her father and his actions affect her as much as she was letting them right now. She was thirty-one. No longer a child. He couldn't control her. And no matter what Riley or even Robot thought—she knew deep down her father would never harm her.

She'd gone to college. She lived by herself in one of the busiest cities in the United States. She was no shrinking violet. When she'd decided to train as a surgeon, she'd vowed she was going to be the best she could be. This little setback wasn't going to alter her goals.

Flinging the covers back she got out of bed, headed to the attached bathroom ready to start the day.

An hour later, travel mug of Riley's amazing coffee

in her hand, Maria released her seatbelt in preparation to exit the car.

A hand on her arm stilled her movements. She looked over to Riley and raised her eyebrow in a silent question.

He reached into his jacket pocket and pulled out a slim black phone. He held it out to her. "Here I want you to use this phone now."

"Why? I've got a perfectly good one."

"A phone which your father knows the number of and, no doubt, is able to trace."

"Oh, okay." She grabbed the phone but Riley tightened his grip and tugged her close. His free hand came up and wrapped around the back of her head.

"This is the first step in keeping you safe. The only numbers programmed into the phone are mine, Tex's and Robot's. If you need anything call any number at any time."

Any time? What did he mean by that?

"Does this mean I'll be going back to my apartment?"

As much as she'd wanted to go back to her home last night, after spending the night at Riley's, the thought of returning to her apartment didn't appeal. If that wasn't a red flag that she was beginning to rely on Riley she didn't know what was.

"No. Until I know for sure that nothing is going

to happen to you, you're staying with me. I'll arrange to get more clothes and other personal items moved to my place today."

"Okay, thanks."

The left side of his mouth rose in half a smile. "No argument?"

"What would be the point?" she responded with a grin. "It would only fall on deaf ears."

The half grin became a full blown one and her heart skipped a beat. "Doc, is learning. Now, have a good day and if you want to have lunch, call me." He leaned forward and kissed her lightly on the lips. The connection was too short for her. If the car behind them hadn't sat on their horn, she would've wrapped her arm around his neck and deepened the kiss.

"Guess I'd better go."

"Yes, you should."

Her hand grasped the handle and she opened the door. "Have a good day, *Ash*."

With his laughter ringing in her ears, and a lightness in her step she entered the hospital ready to face whatever the day would bring.

If someone told her twenty-four hours ago that she would put her life in the hands of a man she'd met once, she would've laughed in their face. Was it wrong to give her trust over to Riley so quickly or was it the best thing she'd ever done?

CHAPTER EIGHT

Darkness fell over the city and Riley still hadn't heard from Maria to say she'd finished for the day. After driving her to and from work for the last week, his admiration for her had grown seeing her commitment to her job and saving lives.

The last time he'd checked in with Tex, he'd told him she was still in surgery. Just as he was about to call Tex again, his phone vibrated, the action causing the phone to skitter across the smooth wooden top.

He snatched it up, relief flowing through him when he saw Maria's name flash on the screen.

I'LL BE DONE IN ABOUT FIFTEEN MINUTES.

Short and sweet.

Part of him was a little disappointed, and he had no idea why. Was he expecting her to finish off with *xoxo?* Over the last week they'd fallen into a good routine with each other. There hadn't been any more kisses, but there had been plenty of dreams where he'd woken, hot, hard and sweaty.

He gave himself a mental shake. He was no lovesick sap. Throwing a twenty on the table he strode out of the café and to his car. He would be at the hospital in ten minutes. Pulling out in traffic he accessed his contact list through the cars Bluetooth and hit Tex's name. It didn't even ring twice.

"I've got her, she's in the staff locker room, collecting her gear."

"I'm heading there now. I should be there in ten minutes."

Through the car speakers, Riley could hear the tick-tap of keystrokes. "I've got eyes on her until she gets in your car."

"Sounds good. Any news on the names I gave you today?"

"Yeah, I'll send you an email and you can review it all. They're mostly low riders. Way down on the Moretti family list."

"Damn, I was hoping one of the names might have Giovanni's ear."

"From what I've been able to dig up on the Moretti organization, Vitorrio, the uncle Maria oper- ated on. He's Giovanni's right hand man. Hence why

Giovanni had his daughter perform the surgery on him."

"Makes sense." Riley tapped the steering wheel as he waited for the lights to change. "What are our chances of Moretti actually letting his daughter walk away from the family? For good?"

"Your guess is as good as mine. But stranger things have happened. Maria's been studying for a long time now to achieve her goals. Maybe Giovanni will have an attack of fatherly love and let her go. He would have to know she wouldn't want to do anything he asked of her."

"One can only hope. Maybe Italy can find something out with his family connections. He might be able to give us some insight to the inner workings of mafia families."

"Not sure he'll want to get back in touch with that part of his life. But for you he might."

Tex had a point. Carlos *Italy* Porcelli had been a runner for one of Giovanni Moretti's rivals. He'd saved himself from being sucked down the path to drug use and possible death, by enlisting and becoming a SEAL. He hoped Italy would help get something they could use on Giovanni to free Maria.

The bright lights of the hospital came into view. "I've got to go Tex, I'm pulling up to the hospital."

"I see her in the foyer. Talk to you later."

"Later."

Riley disconnected the call as he pulled to a stop out the front of the hospital. Maria walked toward the double doors, her head down shoulders slumped with her hands stuck in the pockets of the jacket she wore. It was like she had the weight of the world on her shoulders.

What had happened? And why hadn't Tex told him something was up. He grabbed his phone and fired off a quick text to his friend.

DID SOMETHING HAPPENING TO MARIA THAT YOU DIDN'T TELL ME ABOUT.

A second later his phone dinged. He checked the screen and where Maria was.

NO. WHY?

The door opened so he fired off a quick TTYL response and popped his phone back into the inner pocket of his jacket.

The pungent smell of antiseptic filled the car as Maria settled herself in.

"Hey," he said.

"Hey." Her response was quiet and she turned her head to look out the window.

Riley had no idea what was wrong, but even he knew questioning her in the car wasn't a good idea. He'd let her decompress and then when they got home he'd see if he could get to the bottom of what was troubling her.

His first thought was that something happened to someone she'd operated on. He imagined it didn't get any easier when she lost a patient. It hadn't gotten easy for him if one of their missions didn't go as planned and someone got hurt or died. It hadn't happened often, but there had been plenty of times when it had come close.

With a twist of his hands he pulled away from the curb. Using the controls on the steering wheel, he changed the radio to a classical music station, hoping the music soothed her frazzled nerves.

Traffic was heavy so it took them longer than he thought it would to get back to his apartment. By the time he pulled into his building's parking garage the silence in the car was getting to him. He'd restrained himself on numerous occasions from reaching out and placing his hand on Maria's thigh. Or grab her hand as a sign to let her know that he was there for her.

He pulled the car to a stop in his designated bay and shut the engine off. Maria didn't move. She seemed glued to the seat. Sighing, he released his seatbelt and got out of the car. When he reached her side he opened her door. He squatted down and gently placed his hand on her arm.

"Doc, we're home." He practically whispered the words. She showed all the signs of being in shock. More than she had the night she'd almost been knocked over by a car.

"Oh okay." With robotic like movements she grabbed her bag, took off the seatbelt and climbed out of the car.

Riley wrapped an arm around her waist and closed the door. He kept her tight against him until they got into his apartment and he seated her on the couch.

What would she have done if he hadn't picked her tonight?

She'd have gone home to an empty apartment where she would've dealt with whatever had happened to her by herself. That's what would've happened.

Sitting next to her he grabbed her hands in his. "Talk to me, Maria. What happened today?"

A shudder ripped through her body and he gathered her close, baffled at what was happening to the strong woman he knew her to be.

"It was awful."

"What was awful, Doc?"

"It's not the first time I've lost a patient. I mean I know I can't save everyone it's impossible. Sometimes their injuries are too much. Sometimes you do a simple surgery. There's an underlying issue that hadn't been picked up on and you lose them."

Not for the first time he admired her for her choice of occupation.

"Did that happen today? A simple surgery that went wrong?"

"No. Although it might have been easier to deal with if it had been." She looked up at him, her brown eyes dulled with the emotional pain she was going through. "He had his whole life ahead of him. He shouldn't have been in the operating theater today. He should've been at the park playing with his friends."

Oh fuck, a child. She'd lost a child.

"What was wrong with him?"

"He'd been stabbed by the sick fuck who was supposed to be his father. Oh my God, Riley, every time we sewed a laceration up and thought we had a chance, another bleeder would be found."

"Oh, Doc, I'm so sorry." He pressed a kiss on her head. "I believe you did absolutely everything you could to save him."

Tears filled her eyes. "I did, I really did. I don't think I'll ever forget the sound of his mom's wailing when I told her, her son didn't make it."

He held her as the tears she'd been holding at bay poured out of her. He'd heard the type of wail she was talking about at funerals he'd attended for fallen SEALs. Even the hardest of soldiers were affected by the cries of a mother or wife, even fathers, over the loss of their loved one. Riley knew it would be a long time, if ever, before Maria could put that sound out of her mind.

Her crying slowed down until she shuddered every now and then. What she needed was some wine and a warm bath. He wasn't used to emotional females, but he'd heard, from the various girls that had hung of him and his team when they'd gone to bars, that baths and wine went a long way to healing hurts.

"Hey, stay here I'm going to fix you something that will make you feel better." He felt her nod and kissed her again on the top of her head.

Walking into the kitchen he pulled a bottle of white wine out of the refrigerator. The cork popped out and he poured the straw colored liquid into a glass. When he walked back into the living room, Maria had moved from the couch and was gazing out the window looking at the view. He stopped behind her and lightly tapped her on her shoulder.

"I've got you some wine."

"I don't want anything to drink." There was none of the usual sass in her tone. He found he didn't like it. He wanted to see the feisty Maria back, but he also could understand the reason why she was hiding. Hopefully after her wine and bath, she'd feel a little better.

"Well I'll just leave it on the table."

Her nod the only sign she'd heard him, he backed out of the room leaving her to her thoughts.

Was this how she always acted after she lost a patient? Or was this more significant because it was a young child and had happened while her life was in turmoil with her father.

Once Maria was in her bath he was going to call Tex and see if he'd seen anything on the cameras. He knew his friend couldn't watch Maria all the time, hell the guy was probably watching Wolf's team ladies or doing the other stuff for the military. Not to mention spending time with Melody and his girls. He should probably leave it, it wasn't like Tex could do anything anyway.

A few minutes later he walked back into the room, Maria still stood where he left her, the glass of wine untouched.

Okay, he'd given her space. Given her time with her thoughts. But if she was going to get back into that theater tomorrow, she needed to snap out of it. He'd seen this with some guys on base when they'd seen some of the atrocities the men in Afghanistan had done to their women.

"Maria," he spoke low, but firmly.

No reaction. Nothing seemed to penetrate the shell she'd erected around herself. He marched over to her. Instead of stopping behind her, he stepped in front of her.

"Maria, you need to come with me." Riley took hold of one of her hands. They were icy cold. "Let's go."

As they passed the coffee table he scooped up the wine glass and led her to the bathroom. While he wasn't adverse to the idea of undressing her, he was pretty sure that once Maria snapped out of her stupor she wouldn't appreciate him being so forward.

They entered the guest bathroom. A subtle rose fragrance lingered in the air. Thank goodness his housekeeper had set up the room with everything a guest would like, including rose scented bubble bath.

Riley placed her glass of wine on the edge of the bath, before turning to smooth Maria's jacket off her.

"What are you doing?" Hands latched onto his, her fingernails digging into the top of his hands.

"Taking your jacket off."

"I can see that. Would you like to tell me why?"

It was impossible to hold back his smile. "Ahh you're back with us, I see."

He couldn't deny he was happy she'd snapped herself out of her stupor. He'd been worried she wouldn't be able to get herself together in time for work the next day.

"That still doesn't explain why you were taking my jacket off."

"I would've thought it was obvious." He pointed the foamy bath. "You can't have a bath while fully dressed."

"You drew me a bath?" There it was, the spark that had been missing in her eyes since he'd picked her up from work was back.

Score one for Team Riley.

"Yes. And I got you wine." As much as he wanted to stay, to make sure she didn't fall back into her pit of despair, he backed away from her. "I'll leave you to enjoy your bath and get started on dinner."

"You're going to cook me dinner? No take out tonight?"

He couldn't help but smile. Yes, over the last week it had been easier to order food. It hadn't been his plan to cook, but when was the last time someone had looked after her? Probably a long time ago. Or never given who her father was. Tonight he was going to be the one to take care of her.

The wetness glistening in her eyes was his undoing. He closed the gap between them. "Yeah, Doc. I'm gonna cook you dinner."

Giving into temptation he lowered his lips until

they met hers. He groaned at her sweet taste and the tentative way she opened beneath him. This wasn't his best idea, but it was one he wasn't going to argue with himself over. The need to reassure her that she was special overruled any of his self-imposed regulations of dealing with a client.

Maria was worth breaking rules for.

CHAPTER NINE

Sleep was proving to be a bitch. Maria tossed the covers back and padded over to the window. She pulled back the drapes and gazed out over the city. Even in the middle of the night the city still hummed with life.

God, how she wanted to sleep, but her brain wouldn't switch off. If she closed her eyes she alternated seeing the distraught features of the mother of the young boy she couldn't save. Or she re-lived the kiss with Riley over and over again.

He'd been amazing tonight. A quiet strength she hadn't known she'd needed in her life. He'd looked after and even though she knew he wanted to get her to talk about what had happened at work, he'd kept quiet.

Disappointment had flowed through her when

he'd retreated to his study to work after he'd cooked her a delicious meal. She yearned to feel his arms around her again. To recreate that feeling of security and protection she'd experienced while they'd been kissing. Her body had come alive under his touch.

What would it feel like if he made love to her? If he kissed his way down her body like the way he'd kissed her tonight. What would it feel like to have that every night? To have someone care and protect her so she wouldn't have to worry about her father or the family coming after her.

It was a wild dream. A dream that would never come true. There was no man on earth who would want to get involved with her. Not with who her father was. Regardless of what Riley, Tex and anyone else who had an opinion, she would be better off going back to her father. Then everyone else could get on with their lives and not be tainted by her or her drama.

God, I'm throwing my own pity party.

She hadn't gotten this far in life by letting a little adversary set her back. Why was she allowing it to get to her now?

What she needed was sleep. A goodnight's sleep and everything would seem better. She hoped.

Turning, she screamed when she spied the dark shadow standing two feet away from her.

Strong hands grabbed her shoulders and she's immediately kicked the shins of her would be assailant.

"Doc. Stop. It's me. Riley."

His voice penetrated the haze of fear buzzing through her ears. "Riley?" She hit his shoulder then. "What the hell do you think you're doing sneaking up on me? Haven't you heard of knocking?"

"I was coming to check on you. See if you needed anything or if you were okay. And I didn't knock because I didn't want to wake you in case you were sleeping. You need your rest."

"As you can see I'm not sleeping."

She also became aware her hand rested on his shoulder. His firm, unclothed shoulder. A quick glance down confirmed Riley was shirtless and only had on a pair of shorts that hung low on his hips. In the muted light she could see the defined outline of his six-pack. The tattoo covering part of his chest intrigued her with its almost Aztec look. Did it have a special meaning to him?

Attraction stronger than anything she'd ever known before had her swaying toward him. Her hand reached out and ran slowly down the ridges of his chest. Gooseflesh broke out over his skin. She didn't think it was from the air conditioning.

"What are you doing, Doc?"

"I need to feel like my life is worthwhile. Like I'm worthwhile to someone."

Warm hands covered hers, plastering them to his hot flesh. "You are worthwhile. What you do every day is worthwhile. You save lives, Maria. Don't ever think you're not worth something to someone. Every single family member appreciates and is thankful for what you do."

"That's my job. It's what I do. But growing up with my father, I could never have real friends. Who would want to be friends with the daughter of a mobster? Plus my father vetted pretty much all my friends. After a while I stopped trying to make friends, it was safer. So yeah, I don't feel like I'm worthwhile."

Maria wanted to walk away, but as though he sensed her urge, he tightened the hold he had on her hands. She looked up at him, shocked at the intensity of his gaze. His eyes sparked fire and she wasn't sure if it was anger or desire burning in their depths. Not wanting to hope he felt the growing attraction between them like she did, she went with believing he was angry. A thought immediately disregarded when his hands smoothed over her shoulders and he leaned down, stopping millimeters from her mouth.

"I think you're worthwhile," he whispered as he

closed the minuscule gap and placed his lips over hers.

A sigh emanated from her and her arms closed around his waist, reveling in the feel of his warm, hard body beneath her fingers.

Today wasn't the first time she'd lost a patient. But it was the first time she had someone who she could lean on. Someone who could make her feel again. Like life meant something.

Riley pulled her closer, deepening the kiss and his hard length pushed against her belly. An answering wetness pooled between her thighs.

It was insane how attracted she was to a man she'd only known for a couple of weeks. Her fingers trailed from his back to his front until she reached the hard ridge of his flesh. Feeling bolder than she ever had before, her fingers gripped him through the soft cotton fabric of his shorts.

His groan emboldened her to stroke his engorged flesh. His lips pulled away from hers and she moaned her disappointment.

"Doc, I don't think we should be doing this."

Embarrassment washed over her and she pulled her hand away and stumbled from him.

Had she misread him? Misread the whole kiss? It had been so long since she'd been involved in any sort of relationship, but she still understood the male anatomy and from the way his flesh seemed to get harder in her hand, she knew Riley had to be attracted to her. Plus he *kissed* her. He'd made the first move. Now he was saying they shouldn't be kissing?

Wrapping her arms around herself, she looked up at him. The answer to the questions rattling around her mind were reflected in his eyes, desire still burned brightly.

"This doesn't make sense, you want me, and I want you. What's the issue?" Blurting her thoughts out had never been her intention, but she wasn't ashamed of it.

When he took two steps away from her, he may as well have taken twenty. "You're right, I do want you. But you've had a tough day. I don't want you to wake up with regrets, and that's exactly what I think you'll do if we keep doing what we were doing."

"Oh my God, that's the most absurd thing I've ever heard. I'm pretty sure I wouldn't have any regrets."

"Are you sure about that? I have no doubt any other guy would take advantage of you right now. You had an emotional day at work. You were basically in a trance for an hour after I picked you up. Your life is in turmoil because your father tried to have you knocked down or kidnapped again a week ago. Tell me how us sleeping together would be a good thing?"

"Because if I'm going to die I want at least to have a good memory."

The confession burst out of her. Saying out loud the possibility of her dying was sobering, not only to her, but to Riley as well. He moved back to her faster than a bolt of lightning was any indication.

His warm hands curled around her upper arms. "Not on my watch. I'm not going to let anything happen to you, Doc."

"You can't guarantee that."

"Life doesn't come with guarantees, but I do. Trust me."

The assurance should've made her feel better. She still wasn't convinced he could keep his word.

"I want to believe you. I really do, but you don't know my father."

"And you don't know me. Once a SEAL always a SEAL. I may not be a member of my team anymore. But, between them, me, and my business partner Storm, nothing is going to happen to you. We will find a way to get you away from your family."

Her eyes closed as his fingers traced lightly down her cheek. Her own hand reached out and landed on his bare chest again.

She wanted this. She wanted to make love to Riley. How could she regret it in the morning? He was here in front of her.

Strong.

A silent warrior who'd faced many difficult things while he'd been a SEAL. If he said he could help and keep her safe. Then she believed him.

"I trust you, Ash."

If she hadn't had her hands on his chest she never would've felt the slight hitch at her calling him by his nickname. The only other time she'd called him by that she'd said it sarcastically.

"Do you think you'll be able to sleep now?"

Fatigue brushed its fingers over her body.

"I guess."

When Riley's warm lips landed on hers it was the last thing she'd been expecting. But she wasn't going to complain. Wanting to prolong the contact, she slid her hand up his chest over, his shoulder and inched around his neck.

A sigh escaped her as he pulled his lips away from hers.

"Night, Doc."

She didn't want him to leave, but everything pointed to him keeping his word and not taking advantage of her. "Night, Ash."

CHAPTER TEN

K*eep walking.*

Keep walking.

The phrase played over and over in his mind as he walked away from Maria's room, heading straight for his bathroom and a cold shower.

It had been the right thing to do to stop things progressing from bad idea territory to monumentally bad idea territory.

They'd already shared too many kisses. Never before had he gotten involved with someone he'd been assigned to protect. Never had wanted to, so what was it about Maria that made him want to throw all caution to the wind?

With this job as a SEAL he'd never given any thought to having a serious relationship with anyone. Being deployed for months on end with the threat of losing his life around any corner didn't make let's-get-married a priority for him. He'd vowed once he enlisted he wouldn't put a woman through worry of never know if he'd come home or not. Not that he'd found any woman he loved. Until maybe now.

He forced his mind down on that thought. It was impossible to think he loved Maria. Apart from the fact he'd only known her a couple of weeks. They hadn't spent nearly enough time together to get to know each other. Although it hadn't been a burden to have her living in his house. Doing things couples do, like eating together, watching tv shows, and sharing a few hot kisses. All of that together didn't equal true love, though.

How about the fact that you've never shared kisses with anyone like the ones you've shared with Maria?

That little voice needed to shut the hell up.

He reached his room, the shower beckoning. Although he could think of better ways to relieve the hard-on he was still sporting. Namely, turning around and walking back the direction he'd just come from. The chance of being turned away was slim, not with the way Maria had wanted him to take the next step. His body wanted him to take the next step. His sense of honor told him not to because Maria was vulnerable. Had been through so much and he couldn't take advantage of her.

It wouldn't be fair.

"Fuck." The word exploded out of him as he moved toward the shower, shucking his shorts, leaving them in a heap on the tiled floor.

With a flick of his wrist the water shot out of the shower head. He turned the dial toward the "C", grit his teeth and got in. The sting of the cold water struck his skin like a hundred needlepoints. He was too damn old for cold showers, but it was having the desired effect and he'd gone from full mast to quarter mast. He switched the water to warm and quickly washed himself.

As he dried himself his mind went over what he needed to do. He needed to check in with Tex and find out what he'd managed to find out about Maria's father and the *family* business. Also Italy had sent him a text to say he would be meeting with someone from his past who might be able to help them in this situation.

Those were the things he needed to concentrate on. Not on Maria. Not on the way she'd felt in his arms. Not on the way his body wanted to lose himself in her.

"Stop." He spoke the command out loud in the vain hope it would halt his thoughts from hurtling down the road they were on at breakneck speed.

He tossed the towel to the ground and stomped

into his room, coming to an abrupt halt at the sight
that greeted him.

Maria.

In his bed.

Looking at him as if he was a steak dinner and she
hadn't eaten in months. In an instant he went back
from quarter mast to full mast.

"What are you doing here?" He ground the words
out as he turned his back on her and headed for his
dresser to get something to put on.

"I couldn't sleep. I need you, Riley."

His hand gripped the handle of the drawer he was
about to pull open. The need in her voice reached out
and wound itself around the need he'd been trying so
desperately to deny.

"This really isn't a good idea, Doc."

The rustle of his bed covers gave him a few
seconds warning. Enough to brace himself for what
was about to happen next.

It hadn't been enough. Warm hands smoothed
up his back, over his shoulders, stopping on his
belly. The sensation of her naked body pressed
against his back could only be described as
subliminal.

Anything he'd been about to say flew out of his
mind as her hands traveled further south and gripped
his engorged flesh.

"You want this as much as I do. Don't deny it. Your body doesn't lie."

Her fingers stroked from the base to the tip of his penis. Of their own volition his eyelids drifted down as she maintained a slow pace.

He could stay like this forever. Maria's body warming his back, her hand working magic on him.

A shudder rippled through him when her lips traced across his shoulder. He could quite easily pop his load right now. But he didn't want to. He only wanted to do that buried deep inside of her.

The war within him was over. Surrender wasn't something he did often, but surrender to Maria and her desires was what he did right now.

Turning quicker than a bullet finding its target, he had his arms wrapped tightly around her, his cock brushing against her belly. Bending a little at the knees he scooped her up and carried her over to his bed. Not wanting to break contact, but knowing he had to if he wanted to lay her on the bed and not crush her.

He did exactly that, lay her down as though she was made of spun gold. A very precious metal that should be cherished.

Sprawled on the bed in front of him, he let himself look at her for the first time. Her dark hair spread out against his grey sheets. Her mouth slightly plump from his kisses. He climbed on the bed next to her, lying on his side so he could look his fill. She was beautiful. Her breasts full and enticing him to touch and taste them. Her belly, slightly rounded, leading to the place he couldn't wait to sample. Her neatly trimmed dark curls hid the most precious part of her.

"You're so beautiful," he whispered reverently as his hand followed the path his eyes had just taken. He cupped one breast, catching her nipple between his thumb and forefinger. Lowering his head, he traced his tongue around her areola, before taking her hardened peak into his mouth. Her body arched up at the contact.

Oh how he wanted to go slow. Savor every touch and taste every inch of her. It was impossible though. This one sweet taste of her flesh only drove the need in him to join their bodies.

He moved over her so that he lay on top of her, his cock resting between her legs. They were made for each other.

The thought floated through his mind and took purchase. He liked the idea a lot. He liked the idea of protecting Maria for the rest of his life. Picking her up after her day at work. Consoling her if she lost a patient, celebrating the victories as well.

Now he knew why Storm had thrown caution to the wind when he'd gotten involved with Lily. When the right woman came along, and no matter how quickly it happened, you would do everything in your power to be with them.

He rested his weight on his elbows so he could frame her face with his hands. Looking deeply into her eyes, he made a silent vow that he would do whatever it took to free Maria from her family.

While he'd been in Afghanistan he'd faced men holding grenades out toward him and survived. He could survive the steps necessary to give the woman looking up at him with desire burning brightly in her eyes, the one thing she craved the most. Her freedom and the will to do with her life whatever she wanted.

He closed the distance between them and kissed her, putting every one of his emotions into this one touch. A sigh left her and her arms tightened around his neck. His erection nudged her entrance, sliding into her would be easy to do. One pump of his hips and he'd be inside her.

Protection.

At least one part of his brain was still aware of what was happening and not lost in the haze of cravings.

Riley broke the kiss and rolled off her to the opposite side of the bed.

"Where are you going?" A finger poked him in the back.

"Protection." He replied as he opened the drawer and pulled a box of condoms out and emptied the contents onto the table.

"Oh."

Riley grabbed a foil packet and ripped it open with his teeth. "Did you think I was going to walk away?" he asked as he rolled the rubber on.

"You did once before."

That was true, he had walked away from her. Gathering her close, he rotated them so that she lay on top of him. "I'm not going anywhere." He lifted his hips, reinforcing her words. There was no way in hell he could or would walk away from her now.

A wicked gleam entered her eyes and she leaned forward and nipped his bottom lip. Sensation arrowed straight down to his already engorged flesh. With their changed positions, he'd been happy to let her take the lead. Now, not so much. Threading his fingers through her hair he cupped her skull and sought out her lips once again. He turned them again so that he was back on top. With his mouth occupied he reached down between her legs and stroked her slick folds, her body arched into his. Holding back was impossible. The need to own her couldn't be denied.

Pulling his lips from hers he gazed into her smoky

eyes. Her cheeks glowed with a tinge of pink. She was gorgeous and she was his.

Possessiveness he'd never felt before burned through him as he entered her with one swift stroke. Her breath hissed out against his cheek and he stilled, enjoying the sensation of her warm inner muscles clutching at him. He could stay like this forever.

"Is everything okay?" she whispered.

Riley pressed his lips close to her ear. "Every thing is perfect."

He started to move in earnest then, long strokes in and out. Maria raised her hips, chasing him every time he pulled out. The nerves in his feet began to tingle. The sensation rising up his legs and he knew his release was imminent.

Fingernails dug into his back, and his control almost shattered. He lowered his head and captured one of her nipples in his mouth, sucking deeply. It was enough to send Maria over the edge and her orgasm rocketed through her. The sweet bite of her muscles, clenching and releasing him as he continued to move within her, set his own release in motion. He peppered kisses down her jaw as his body pulsed inside of her.

Nothing could be better than this.

CHAPTER ELEVEN

Maria caught another side-eye from one of her colleagues as she walked down the hallway toward the stairwell. It probably had to do with the smile on her face. A smile she'd had since Riley dropped off at work and kissed her with an intensity that had her wanting to forget about work and go back to his place and climb back into bed with him.

Waking up, wrapped in his arms had been an amazing feeling. Never before had she'd spent the night in someone's arms. It had been torture to tear herself out of them. Riley had seemed reluctant to let her go as well. She'd been eating breakfast at the small table in his kitchen when he'd walked into the room, a frown etched into his face. His refusal to answer any questions should've bothered her. Everything in her screamed that whatever had caused that frown had everything to do with her and her family.

The drive to work had been tense and then he'd kissed her and all her doubts and coherent thoughts had evaporated.

So what if she was smiling when she usually kept her smiles to a minimum. Today was going to be a good day.

"You're in a good mood. I wonder why that is?" The voice lowered an octave. "Did someone get lucky last night? Are you getting protection with benefits?"

A shiver of fear trickled down her spine. She knew that voice. Had heard it many times before escaping her father's house.

Andre Zampatti, her father's enforcer, the man who'd been driving the car that had almost hit her.

She knew one thing though; she wasn't going to let her fear show. No fucking way.

Maria straightened her spine and swiveled on her clog-clad feet. "Get the fuck away from me."

His hand grabbed her upper arm in a vice like grip. "Watch your mouth. Now you and I are going for a little drive." He encouraged her to keep going down the stairs.

Her attempts at releasing his hold on her were futile. With every shake of her arm, the tighter he grasped.

"It would be a good idea, Maria, not to fight me. You don't want to have an unfortunate accident, do you?

How had he known where to find her? How had he known she was about to take the stairs instead of the elevator to the cafeteria? It wasn't what she normally did. The stairs were the one place where she would be alone and vulnerable. Was Tex watching? Did this concrete cavern even have cameras in it? And where was Riley? Did he go work another case when she was working?

"Your daddy is going to be very pleased to see you. He's missed his little *petalo*."

Petal!

No way was she her father's *petal*. Never had been and had no plans to be one either. Giovanni Moretti would not crush her.

When they reached the door leading to the parking garage Andre halted before opening it. He reached down and pulled out a black plastic bag that been placed behind the trashcan. A trashcan that didn't normally reside in the stairwell.

Before she had time to ask him, Andre peeled off her white coat and threw it into shiny silver receptacle.

"What do you think you're doing? Those coats aren't cheap you know." A coarse sweater was pulled over her head. Reflexively she pushed her arms through the armholes. A ball cap was shoved on top of her head.

"Let's go." He slung an arm around her shoulder and opened the door. Andre kept his head low and angled toward hers. She knew, from when she'd almost been run down, that there were cameras in the parking garage. Clearly, Andre knew this as well, hence the butt-ugly pea green sweater she now wore, along with the hat and the way he shielded himself and her from the cameras.

Could she give Tex a signal that it was her being ushered through the parking garage? He had to know she wasn't in surgery. Or with a patient. Or in the cafeteria, where she had been headed to when Andre had caught her and whisked her away.

Maria had no time to even raise her arm as a she was hustled into a car quicker than a squirrel scampering across a road.

If Tex was watching the screens would he notice their getaway? God, she can't believe she was putting so much hope on Tex doing nothing but sitting in front of screens watching her. He had a family. One of the girls could be sick. Or he could be taking Mel to an appointment. And Riley, where was he?

For the first time since she'd performed surgery on her uncle, she was wishing she worked in a different occupation. One where it would be possible to have Riley sitting at a desk next to her. Going to get a coffee when she did. But it was all wishful think-ing. And in a situation like this wishful thinking would get her nowhere. She needed to remain calm and hope there was a way she could let Riley and Tex know her whereabouts.

Riley.

Her heart ached at the thought of never seeing him again. If she was correct in her assumption of where she was being taken, getting her away would be near on impossible. Would she never have the oppor-tunity to explore the chance of a relationship with Riley now? She didn't want to only spend one night in his arms. He made her feel safe. With him she knew she didn't have to always be the strong one. They hadn't spent that much time together, but somehow she knew that he would be perfect for her. She didn't want it be over before it had truly begun.

No matter what, she would fight with everything she had; she would get back to him. Their story had only just begun.

"Where are you taking me?" The question didn't need to be asked as she really did know her final destination. The large compound in Jersey where her father lorded over everyone. Ironic the biggest mafia boss in New York lived in New Jersey.

"Never you mind. You'll find out when we get there. Now I think it's time you had a nap."

What did he mean for her to take a nap? The sharp sting of a fine needle piercing the skin registered.

"Shit." Was the only word she could manage before a black veil descended upon her.

Now she was scared.

"Why is she still out? What did you do to my daughter, Andre? If you've harmed her in anyway you will pay."

Through the layers of fog currently in her mind, Maria recognized her father's voice. Her stomach roiled as the haze began to fade away. The last thing she wanted to do was vomit at her father's feet, but maybe he deserved it after everything he'd done to her. She breathed through her nose and out through her mouth in an attempt to still her stomach.

Her father still ranted, but it was background noise as her focus was all on making sure she didn't toss her cookies. After a few seconds her stomach settled.

"Shut up, Papa."

Papa.

Old habits died hard. At one point in her life he had been her *Papa*. Now he was just the man who she shared DNA with.

"Are you all right, *dolcezza*? Do you need anything?"

Sweetie?

He called her sweetie? The man was delusional to think he had a right to call her that.

"I'm not your *Sweetie*," she blurted out as she struggled from a reclining position to sitting. The room whirled around her. She closed her eyes, counted to five before opening them again. Thankfully the room had stopped moving like a spinning top.

Her father reached out a hand to place on her forehead. She recoiled from his touch. A flash of hurt passed through his eyes, so quick she was sure she'd imagined it.

"Can I get you a drink?" This time, his tone was formal, like he would use when addressing a guest.

"Water." Her throat was dry and she knew it would be that way for a couple of hours, until the drug that had been used to sedate her was truly out of her system. If she had to guess what drug she'd been given she would have to go with something along the lines of Propofol.

A glass of iced water appeared in front of her,

pulling her from her rumination about what had been injected into her system.

Taking a small sip she chanced a look around the room. Nothing looked familiar to her. There was no picture of the Sicilian port on the wall. Nor was the sofa she was sitting on the rose pink suede one she had sat on when she was a kid. Instead she sat on a white leather sofa. So unless her father had demolished the house she'd grown up in and completely rebuilt and refurnished it in the ten years since she'd last ventured inside, it seemed she'd been taken to a place she'd never visited before.

"Where am I? And you still haven't answered why I'm here and why you felt it necessary to kidnap me? Your own daughter. Your *dolcezza*."

If she expected her father to show any remorse for actions she was wishing for a pipe dream. His face remained impassive. No hint of shame or apology for what he'd done to her.

The concern she heard in his voice as she struggled to regain consciousness must have been a dream. False concern because obviously he needed her for something, and if she'd been rendered into a permanent catatonic state her usefulness would be zero.

"I've missed you."

Three words. That was his explanation? As if that

would make her want to forgive him for the hell he'd put her through recently.

"Forgive me if I don't believe you, father." She took another sip of her water. The gelatinous feeling in her arms and legs was subsiding. She was starting to feel human again.

"You're my daughter. My flesh and blood, why wouldn't I want you close? It's time you came home."

Maria looked around the room again. "This isn't my home. And you agreed to let me lead my own life. To do my own thing."

"And who paid your bills for medical school? Did you think you earned your scholarships?"

Any feeling she had in her legs and arms, drained out of her at her father's confession. Another illusion she had that she'd been independent the last ten years shattered in front of her.

She really had been living in a dream world, and was about to keep dreaming by thinking she and Riley had a chance at a future together. She wasn't a little girl anymore. Dreams didn't come true. Her dream of ever being free would never come to fruition as long as her father was alive.

"What do you want from me?"

CHAPTER TWELVE

"Where the fuck is she, Tex? You were supposed to have eyes on her." Riley paced around his office, agitation and anger vying for top spot.

"I was watching her, but I do have other jobs, Ash. Not to mention other SEAL teams I'm watching. As well as a wife and two daughters."

Riley blew out a frustrated breath. "Yeah I know, Tex. I'm sorry. How are Wolf and the others."

"They're fine."

Riley sat back down at his desk and woke his computer up. The map on the screen still didn't have a blinking light showing Maria's location via the GPS in her cell phone. He knew she kept the phone on her at all times, except when she was in surgery and then it was in her locker. Her phone was always on, so why wasn't it on now.

The burning in his gut intensified as the silence stretched on the phone between him and Tex.

"If only I didn't have to go to that other job today, I could've stayed around the hospital and kept her safe."

"You know you can't live with 'what ifs', brother. It will only do your head in."

Tex was right. It was something he'd come to terms with during his time in Afghanistan. When you had the enemy breathing down your neck and every step you took could potentially end your life, nothing good ever came from boarding the 'what if' train.

"I know. But she's..." he broke off not wanting to voice what he was really thinking.

"Your woman and you will do everything possible to protect her." Tex finished what he couldn't.

"Yeah." He closed his eyes and remembered how Maria had looked this morning, lying asleep in his arms. Even now his heart picked up its pace at how right it had been to hold her. How right she had looked in his bed. In his home. "How the hell did this happen. It's too soon," he muttered.

Tex laughed down the line as he clicked away on his keyboard. "Love doesn't follow any rule books. It's a law unto itself. But it's a law I embrace and never want to let go. When it's right, it's right, Ash. You don't fight love."

Immediately he wanted to object to Tex's declaration that he loved Maria. Hell, they hadn't known each other long at all. It was impossible. Yet how could he explain what he was currently feeling? The desperation coloring his consciousness that he knew wouldn't ease until he had Maria in his arms and where he knew was safe.

Falling in love with her was the only logical explanation, but he wasn't ready to face it yet. The only thing he could focus on right now was getting her back.

"I'm not sure I'm there yet, but I'll take your advice on board."

Again Tex laughed. "You keep on thinking that way."

Wanting to divert the attention off his growing feelings for Maria, Riley directed the conversation back on the matter at hand—determining how the hell Maria's father had got his hands on her. He had no doubt Giovanni Moretti was responsible for Maria's disappearance.

"How did Giovanni manage this, Tex? How could he make her disappear without anyone noticing until she didn't turn up for surgery?"

"I don't know. I'm trying to piece it all together.

The hospital's security system had an outage so it's a bit of a mess. The last look I have of her is as she entered the stairwell on the third floor."

"And if that's not suspicious then I don't know what is. How convenient that the security system should fail and Maria disappears? This was planned and if I'd been doing my job properly this never would've happened."

"And you're going back to 'what ifs' again, Ash. It's almost impossible to shadow her in the hospital. You know that. No matter what we've done, there's always a little gap in our methods. Unfortunately, Giovanni used that gap to his advantage. In all the time we've been watching her, she's never used the stairwell."

Riley could hear the ringing of the office phone. Everything was going on as normal around him. Storm was out as Lily had had her baby a couple of days ago. The new parents were getting acquainted with their daughter. He allowed himself a small smile as he recalled the delight in his friend's face as he talked about the miracle of Ava's birth. Riley was happy for his friend and one day... He tried to block the road his thoughts were traveling down, but it was impossible. The image of him, Maria and a precious little bundle held in her arms assailed his mind.

How he wanted that to be his future. But he needed to find Maria first.

"Ash, I've got something, but I need to call you back."

Tex disconnected before he could ask what the tech specialist had found. He tossed his phone on the desk and his office phone rang a second later.

"What?" he barked into the receiver he'd snatched up quickly.

"Sorry to bother you, Riley, but there's a person by the name of Italy here to see you?"

The confusion in his assistant's voice was a plain as the nose on his face. "Send him in."

Riley stood and walked to his office door. He looked out and saw his former SEAL team member striding down the hallway, a smile breaking out over his face.

"Man, it's good to see you," Riley said as he pulled Carlos *Italy* Porcelli into a one-armed bro hug.

"You too, Ash. I can see that you're not getting soft in retirement." Italy lightly punched Riley in his abs.

"Never. Come and take a seat."

Riley hoped that Italy had uncovered something in Giovanni's past that could be used against him.

The moment he sat down he laid the envelope

he'd been holding on the table. "I've got some information for you."

Riley reached out and picked up the object. "There's been a development today."

"What's happened?"

Pulling out the sheaf of papers Riley glanced over at the other man. "Maria was taken from the hospital this morning."

"How the hell did that happen? Has Tex been able to get a fix on her location yet?"

Ignoring the papers he'd pulled out of the envelope, Riley sat back in his chair. "It was a combination of life getting in the way of an operation, and Maria doing something she's never done before. You know how it goes. You can never factor in all scenarios when working a mission."

"Ain't that the truth? What about Robot and T-Rex, weren't they supposed to be helping out as well?"

"Yeah. I had them following up on something else for me at the time. As I said it was a perfect storm and we got caught in the vortex. No matter how prepared we were it wouldn't have made a difference. They wanted her badly, and we aren't talking amateurs here. As you know the people we're dealing with and who took her are professional at making people disappear without a trace."

Riley knew he didn't need to say anything more.

Italy would get the drift.

"Her father."

He nodded and picked the papers up again to read them. As he scanned the pages he couldn't believe what he was reading. Although he shouldn't be surprised as to how far a mobster would go to get what he needed done.

He laid the papers back down and eyeballed Italy. "Are you sure this legit? Everything here is the truth?"

Italy squirmed in his seat and Riley's interest was piqued. A SEAL never squirmed. What was up with that?

"Yep, it's 100% legit. And don't ask me how I got the information. Just know that I had to call in a favor and I know that payback, when it comes, will be a bitch."

As much as he wanted this information on Maria's father, the last thing he wanted was for Italy to get caught back in the snare of the life he'd worked hard to leave behind.

"Whatever you need I'll be there for you. No questions asked." No way would he let Italy face the payback by himself. He owed the guy for getting vital information that would help Maria. If they found her.

Riley squashed that thought before it became the truth. What he had to believe was that Tex would get a lead and they would be able to get Maria back.

While at the same time, ensuring her freedom once and for all.

"I'll be fine, Ash."

Italy's confidence should've been all Riley needed to know that he spoke the truth. But an instinct, one honed and never ignored when he'd been on the team, warned him to not take his words lightly.

What had him asking Italy to go back to his past cost the other man?

Before he could question his former teammate more, his cell rang and Tex's name flashed on the screen. He engaged the call and put it on speaker so Italy could hear the conversation.

"What you got for me, Tex? Any news on Maria's location? Italy's here with me too."

"Hey Italy, I got the information you sent me."

Riley looked at him, raised his eyebrow in question. Italy flicked his eyes down to the papers on the desk and back up again. Riley got the message. He appreciated Italy's foresight. It was always good to have a back up copy of information as sensitive as what was on the papers in front of him.

God, it was in situations like this that he missed working with a team. Although he enjoyed being his own boss and now in partnership with Storm and the business had grown from strength to strength, there still was nothing like being part of a tight knit team.

He wondered how the two team members who'd replaced him and Storm were fitting in. No doubt the other guys would've given them a tough initiation.

A poke on his arm pulled him from the tangent his thoughts had floated down. Why the hell was he even thinking about such stuff when his woman was in danger?

"What else do you have for us, Tex?"

"Okay. I managed to get some footage. It's pretty scrambled, but two people exited the stairwell that Maria went into on the third floor."

"You told me she was in the stairwell alone."

"Affirmative. No one followed her in so that means someone was waiting for her."

"How the hell would they know she'd take the stairs?" Riley asked. "It doesn't make sense, she never takes the stairs. So it can't have been luck there was someone waiting for her. Fuck." Realization sank in.

"Yes. It means her father has been watching her as well."

Riley shook his head. His whole business reputation was based upon how fucking good he was at his job. At the way he could protect people. If word got out that someone he'd been tasked to protect had been kidnapped right out from under his nose, he could kiss his business reputation goodbye. He for sure didn't think Storm would be happy with that.

"Look Ash. My guess is Giovanni has someone on the hospital staff on his payroll. It doesn't matter if you were shadowing Maria's every move, we're talking about the Moretti Mob here they were determined to get her and they did."

"I promised her, last night, that nothing would happen to her on my watch. The very next day she gets grabbed. I don't care if Moretti has the whole staff on his payroll. I shouldn't have let this happen."

"What else were you able to ascertain from the video footage, Tex?" Italy asked.

"From what I can see, they got into a dark sedan. I managed to follow it through the transport camera system and followed it to a compound in New Jersey."

"He's taken her to the family home. Is that what you're telling us, Tex?"

"Nope, Ash, it's not the family home. I'm about to email you the schematics. I've got in touch with Robot and he and the rest of the team are on the way. They should be with you in a couple of hours. In the email there will be a link which will take you to the cameras inside the compound perimeter."

The need to see for himself that Maria was safe bubbled inside of him. "What about inside the house? Are there cameras there?"

"Negative, which surprises me. Maybe the man

likes to have privacy inside his home."

"How secure is this place, Tex?" Italy asked the question that Riley had been about to.

"As I can't get eyes inside the house I can't be sure how many are guarding Giovanni and Maria. But on the outside you've got four teams of two men. The property isn't as large as I expected. But that doesn't mean there aren't silent alarms in the unpatroled areas plus other surprises. I'm trying to find out what I can and when I do I'll email it through."

"Thanks, Tex."

"Go get your girl, Ash."

Tex disconnected the call and Riley sank down in his chair. At least he knew where Maria was. He only hoped she hadn't been hurt. If she had been, he wouldn't hesitate to hurt anyone who laid a finger on her.

"Don't worry, Ash. Once the guys get here we will work out a plan and do what we have to do to get her out of there."

Italy's words should've reassured him, but he couldn't help but wonder what they were up against. It couldn't be worse than anything they hadn't experienced on their other missions. Even though he hadn't been a part of the team for five years, he hadn't lost his skills.

Italy was right. They would get her out of there.

CHAPTER THIRTEEN

W ell at least her prison had a nice view. The only consolation to being locked up like a petulant teenager who broke curfew. Her father hadn't told her why he'd brought her to this new house of his. She was still coming to terms with the fact he'd financed her all the way through college and medical school.

Hadn't she earned one of her many scholarships on her own merit? She'd maintained a 4.0GPA average all the way through college. She'd worked her damn butt off through medical school and now she'd just about finished her surgical residency. And everything was a lie?

No.

She refused to believe it was a lie. Her father hadn't sat by her in exams. He hadn't stood by her through all her rotations before she'd settled on being a surgeon. Did it matter that he'd paid for her education. It was what parents were supposed to do. Well, parents who were as rich as her father was.

Maria paced over to the window and looked out over the lush green lawn that led down to the row of trees marking the property's border. She spied the men patrolling. Escape would be impossible for her. No doubt her father had one of his goons guarding her and the moment she walked out the door everyone would be on high alert.

"Riley, are you out there somewhere?" she whispered as she laid a hand the cool glass.

It was wishful thinking. No matter what Tex did, or Riley for that matter. There was no way they could find her.

Why not? You know what Mel's says: Tex can find anyone, even those who don't want to be found.

Maria would bet everything she owned that Tex had never dealt with the Mob before. They were a law unto themselves. She had seen what her father had done over the years. When her mother disappeared she'd become scared, worried that if she spoke the wrong way to her father he would hurt her, too.

The door opened and she turned to see her father standing in the doorway.

"You know it's polite to knock on a closed door

before you enter."

Her father shrugged and stepped into the room, closing the door behind him. Nerves skittered up her spine.

"*Dolcezza*, I'm your father and you're under my roof. I don't need to knock on any door in this house."

Asshole.

She was so tempted to say the word to his face, but maybe it would be better to hear what he actually had to say.

"I guess it's lucky that I wasn't sitting around naked then."

"You've got a smart mouth on you there. Is that how you speak to your supervisors? If so, I'm surprised you're still employed."

"It's a good thing I'm still employed otherwise Uncle Vittorio would be dead."

"He is."

"What?" She had to have misheard or misunderstood his words. "That can't be. He may have been shot three times but when I left him he was holding his own. He should've been fine."

When her father's face remained impassive, she swallowed hard on the ball of fear lodged in her throat.

"You killed him didn't you?"

"He was becoming a liability."

The matter of fact way her father spoke to her shouldn't surprise her. Offing Uncle Vittorio would be the same to him as swatting a fly was to an every day person. Everything started falling into place, but none of it made any sense either.

"You shot him that first time, didn't you?"

"Yes."

Again, no remorse. He had to have some feelings inside of him. At one stage in his life he had to have cared for her mother and for her as well. Or had she and her moth merely been trophies for him.

"Then why the hell did I have to operate on him? Why didn't you let him die then?"

Every instinct she possessed screamed at her to run. Run as far away as possible, only that was never going to happen. With the way her father was acting, if she made any sort of move she could find herself in a similar predicament as her uncle.

Dead.

And dead was the last thing she wanted to be. No way was her father going to rob her of her future with Riley. Whatever that was going to be, she would survive this and have a future with him. She just needed to keep her head in the game.

"Surely by now you know everything I do, I do for a purpose, Maria."

Oh shit, he called her by her proper name. The first time he'd done it since she'd regained consciousness. He'd only ever used her name if he was annoyed with her. Normally he did call her *dolcezza* and she hated it.

But with her resolve to still survive thrumming through her veins, whatever her father had planned for her, she wasn't going to let him intimidate her. Plus she had a few weapons of her own she could use.

"What was your purpose then, Papa?"

Immediately his countenance softened a fraction at her use of *Papa*. Maybe he needed to be reminded that she was his only surviving flesh and blood. That had to count for something. He may have decided her mother wasn't worth his time, but she was his daughter, surely he had some sense of fatherly pride in all that she'd achieved. She hadn't been one of those girls who wanted to mooch off their father. She'd wanted her own career and she'd chosen a damn honorable one, too.

Maybe that was the problem. Perhaps he would've been prouder if she'd wanted to follow him into the family business. Or if she'd been shallow and just wanted to shop and spend all his money on the latest trend. Carry around a puppy in a Chanel purse. By choosing a profession that actually helped people, had she signed her own death warrant?

"In my line of business there are times when going to a public hospital to get treatment isn't an option. I needed to know that my money had been put to good use, hence the little test. Plus there are occasions when time is of the essence. Where locations aren't what you're used to working in. I had to see if you would fulfill my requirements."

"Shooting Uncle Vittorio was a test to see if I would perform for you. If I could perform under pressure and in less than ideal circumstances."

"Yes."

Maria slashed a hand through her hair. "Why can't you let me live my own life, Papa? A life where I don't have to constantly look over my shoulder. If you're worried that I will turn you into the Feds, wouldn't I have done it by now? I mean, hell, after I performed surgery on Uncle Vittorio they knocked on my door the very next day and I gave nothing away."

"I know. And it's not a matter of trust, Maria. It's a matter of who you associate with."

"But I keep mostly to myself. If you've been watching me you would've known that. Please, Papa, let me go. I won't say anything to anyone. I promise."

She hated herself for begging, but maybe it was a way to get through to him. Plus couldn't he tell she wanted nothing to do with this life? Had never wanted anything to do with it.

"I once would've believed that, but recently you've connected with people that may encourage you to go back on your word."

Riley.

He could only be talking about Riley. It was his own fault anyway she'd connected with Riley. If he hadn't pulled her off the street to perform his little test, then she wouldn't have told Mel. Who in turn wouldn't have expressed concerns to Tex and Tex wouldn't have called Riley.

Then you wouldn't have met Riley.

That little voice in her had a point. It was important her father never find out how important Riley was to her. If he did, she had no qualms believing he would harm Riley.

It was imperative that she let her father know that no one made her do anything she didn't want to do.

"Really? You think after all this time I'll let someone influence me and how I act and what I say. If the only way you can get me do something for you is by kidnapping me, I think that would give you a fair indication that I know my own mind."

Before her father could respond everything went dark.

Get down.

Instinct yelled at her and she immediately threw herself on the ground, lying flat.

"Andre." Her father roared. "Maria, where are you?"

She could hear him scrambling around and headed in the opposite direction. She needed to get herself to a place where she wouldn't be in the line of fire. She didn't know how or why, but she knew the reason darkness fell was because of Riley. Hopefully he wasn't on his own. No, he wasn't stupid. He would have his former team with him. They'd promised nothing would happen to her.

Pop. Pop.

"God dammit, girl. How the hell did they find out where we are? Fucking military."

For the first time in her life, the great Giovanni Moretti wasn't the one pulling the strings. Someone else was. And these guys dealt with a shit load of bad guys. If anyone could take him out, they were the ones that could.

"I'd think very carefully before you make a move, Moretti."

Maria recognized the voice even though she didn't think she'd ever heard that tone from Riley before. It was deep, commanding and had a take-no-prisoners element to it. Even she froze in her efforts to put some distance between her and her father.

"What are you going to do, Military Man? Kill me? Wouldn't that go against your military moral code?"

"Here's the thing. I'm no longer in the military, but even if I was, I swore to protect the people of the United States of America from all threats be they foreign or domestic." The sound of the cocking of a gun echoed around the room. "And you, Giovanni, would be considered a domestic threat."

How Riley could remain so cool in a situation like this was beyond her. Her heartbeat raced and blood pounded through her ears.

"You don't have the balls to do it."

What was her father thinking, taunting Riley like that? If she knew anything about military men, well men in general, no one liked to be mocked like that.

"You'd be surprised what Ash can do." The lights flashed on and Maria blinked against the sudden glare. After a second her eyes adjusted and she gasped out loud at the sight that greeted her.

Seven men dressed head to toe in black. Their faces covered in black paint so she had no idea who was who, but they could only be Riley's former SEAL team. She only recognized Riley because he was the one standing with his gun pointed at her father's head.

Maria studied her father's face. If he was frightened he didn't show it. She couldn't see any sweat beading on his forehead. His breathing seemed regular, unlike hers, which was ragged with each breath she took. It almost seemed as though, even with a gun pointed at his head, her father believed he'd get out of this unscathed.

One of the men took a step forwarded to her father. "Oh and if you're wondering about where all your guards are. Let's just say they're sleeping."

Shocked had her standing, Riley's eyes flicked over to her briefly before redirecting his attention back to her father.

"You killed them?"

"No. They're all, as I said, just taking naps."

"Robot?" she asked.

The other man, keeping his eye and weapon trained on her father nodded briefly confirming her suspicion the men were Riley's former teammates.

"Well isn't this lovely. It's a reunion." Sarcasm laced her father's words. This was a side of him he'd never shown her. It was no doubt the side he showed his enemies. The side everyone in New York City knew. "Pity it will probably be the last time you're all together. I will make sure I get every single one of you."

"Is that a threat?" Riley asked. "Because I'm the

one holding a gun at your head not the other way round."

"Whatever you think you can do to me, it won't matter. I will get you."

"Father, stop. I don't know what you're thinking antagonizing these men."

"It's quite simple, *dolcezza,* I'm untouchable. And the sooner this bunch of wanna-bes accept that, the better we'll all be. You're my daughter, Maria. Your place is with me. In this house. In my organization. Your place isn't working for people who don't appreciate you."

A fiery ball of anger burned through her and attempt to get in her father's face, but was halted by one of the SEALS. "You're the one who doesn't appreciate me, Father." She stuck her hands on her hips. "I'm a surgeon. And a damn good one at that. People appreciate everything I do because I *save* lives. I undo the damage that you and your petty mob of assholes wreak on everyone else. I will never, *ever* work for you. Do you understand me? Do what you have to do, Riley. I don't care. I don't have a father anymore."

She turned and went to walk out of the room but was stopped when Robot took hold of her arm. "Let me go," she demanded.

"Wait." He canted his head toward Riley and her

father. "You need to stay."

"It's over, Giovanni. Your days of ruling the streets of New York are done."

Her father, laughed. "I have no idea what you took before you came here, but you're delusional. Even if you somehow get me arrested I'll be back on the streets before you can say *hello*. So do your best solider boy."

Maria held her breath to see what Riley would do. She had no reason not to believe father was saying anything but the truth. Over the years when trouble should've landed at her father's doorstep, it miraculously disappeared and he continued to smell as sweet as a rose. She knew he had police, judges, and other high-ranking officials in his pocket. She guessed he was thinking one of them would get him out of this trouble. Maria knew he shouldn't underestimate Riley and his former team.

Riley's free hand reached up to touch his chest. "Tex, I think we're ready."

A second later the door burst open and shouts of "FBI" echoed around the room. In a blur of movement, Robot had her father on the ground, knee in his back and Riley had her wrapped up in his arms. Her body relaxed immediately into his hold.

Safe.

The word pounded in her mind. She was safe.

CHAPTER FOURTEEN

Riley watched as Maria was questioned by yet another FBI agent. Other agents were moving around her father's office, extracting files from drawers and packing it in boxes for them to take away.

The urge to shoot Giovanni Moretti had been strong. The guy deserved it for not only kidnapping his only daughter, but for all the deaths he'd been instrumental in causing.

The guys had known they couldn't go balls in and get Maria out. They weren't a group of off the grid mercenaries. They were military. So with the information Italy had provided, not only to him but to Tex as well, the decision had been made to bring the Feds into the operation.

The FBI were more than happy to be involved in an operation to bring down one of the biggest mobsters in the United States. They'd be chasing him for years. The information Italy had provided was only the tip of the iceberg. With what the Feds had on Giovanni as well, it had been enough for a raid to be set up, not to mention a rescue operation as well. All they needed was for Giovanni to implicate himself and he'd done that. It was up to the Feds now.

Over time he would pay a couple of visits to Giovanni to make sure he kept his distance from Maria. No way did he want to put her through any more of what she'd been through the few weeks. He'd spoken to Tex about the tracking devices he'd given, to not only Melody and his girls, but also the women and kids on Wolf's team. He would get one for him and Maria. He would do everything in his power to keep her safe.

His Doc.

His love.

The agent who'd been questioning Maria moved away and her shoulders slumped in tiredness. In two quick steps he was by her side.

He pressed a soft kiss to the side of her head as he traced a trail down her arm until he reached her fingers. "Hey, Doc."

A small smile stretched his lips as she swayed into his side. "Get me out of here, Riley. Please."

The request didn't need to be asked twice he scooped her up in arms and strode toward the door.

"Um we will need Ms. Moretti for a little while longer."

Riley turned toward the voice that had spoken. "What? You're going to ask her the same questions the last three agents have all asked her? She's tired. She's been through enough. You're not going to keep her any longer. I'm taking her home."

The agent looked like he was about to protest, but then spied the look in Riley's eyes and backed away. "Right. Well if we need anything we'll be in touch."

"You do that."

Riley continued on his way until they were outside in the night air. He let Maria slide down his body as he released her from his hold, keeping his arms wrapped loosely around her waist.

They stood there for countless moments, both lost in their own thoughts.

A shudder wracked through her and Riley worked out the days event had finally caught up with her and all her emotions were being released by an onslaught of cleansing tears.

His heart ached at all she'd experienced. And it

wasn't just recently, it was a whole lifetime of living with someone who should love and protect her, but wanted her as a pawn in the sick game he called life.

"It's over now, Doc. You're safe, sweetheart. I swear. He won't hurt you again."

"I want to believe that, but you heard him. He's got so many people on his payroll that he will be out before we know it. The moment he is, he'll come after me. I'll never be free."

"Stop," he said and took a step back so he could look into her eyes. The pain and fright dulling them had his anger at her father welling inside of him again. He tamped it down. Getting angry with Giovanni wouldn't solve the issue in front of him. He needed to be calm. If he was calm then hopefully, some of it would radiate toward her and calm Maria as well. "Listen to me. The FBI will make sure he's taken care of. And do you want me to be brutally honest?"

"Yes."

"I'm pretty sure once word gets out on the streets that Giovanni has been caught, all the families who have a beef with him will be chomping at the bit to get their hands on his territory. He'll be lucky if he survives long enough to go to trial."

While he didn't know it for sure, Riley could

imagine that with Giovanni captured by the FBI, no other family in the New York area would want him walking the streets again.

"I hope that's true. I don't ever want to see my father again."

Maria closed the small gap he'd created by stepping away from her and rested her head against his chest once more.

Contentment washed over him. He'd never given a lot of thought of having someone who he could call totally his own, until now. Today when he'd found out she'd been kidnapped he had felt like his heart had been ripped out. Now he understood all that Storm and Tex went on about when they spoke about the women they love. How they would give up their lives for them. How when their women hurt, the hurt was multiplied ten times within them. How the thought of not waking up next to the most important people in their lives crippled them.

Riley understood it all now, because that was how he felt about Maria. He hooked a finger under her chin and raised it until her gaze connected with his.

"I don't ever want to feel what I felt when I found out that you'd been taken today, Doc. The pain inside of me was worse than any bullet wound I've ever had. The thought of anything happening to you brought me to my knees." He smoothed the hair back from her face. "I know it's too soon, and these feelings growing within me are ones I never imagined experiencing in my life. I'm falling in love with you, Maria Moretti. And it feels wonderful."

A breath hiccuped out of her. Her eyes sparkled with the tears she'd shed. "Oh, Riley."

His heart plummeted. Here it came, the *I had a good time last night but I'm not looking for anything serious* speech. What had he been thinking laying his guts out on the table for her to walk all over?

As though she could read his mind her hand cupped his cheek. "No. No, it's not what you're thinking. When I was taken all I could think about was you. How you would be feeling. I knew deep down you'd come and save me, even though I thought it was hopeless. Thoughts of you kept me going the whole time I was in that wretched house. I may have told my father I would do what he wanted, but I wasn't going to. Any chance I had I was going to thwart whatever he wanted me to do. You gave me that strength, Riley. *You.* I'm falling in love with you, too."

Tension raced out of his body like a bullet train racing down the train tracks. He lowered his head and captured her lips with his. Everything he felt for her he poured into the kiss. His fright at her being taken. His pride at how she stood up to her father. And last of all, the burgeoning love he had for her.

When they finally broke apart, their uneven breaths echoed around them.

"Take me home, Riley."

"Always."

EPILOGUE

Laughter rang out around Maria as she sat perched on Riley's lap. His arm rested possessively around her waist. For the first time in her life, Maria belonged to someone. Someone who loved her and cherished her.

Riley had been right, a week after the raid on her father's property, he had been found slumped in the corner of his prison cell. Only it wasn't a rival mob family that had taken him out. It had been his cellmate. A man whose only daughter had been killed by the drugs Giovanni had peddled around New York. It was funny how karma had a way of catching up with you.

"Hey, what's up, Doc?" Maria rolled her eyes at the comment made by Joker, a guy on the SEAL team that had been part of her rescue. With the lame jokes he kept making at the get together to celebrate the birth of Grayson's daughter, Maria had worked out how he got his nickname.

"You need a to be munching on a carrot when you say that to me." She threw back at him. The deep rumble of Riley's laugh reverberated against her back, sending shivers of awareness arcing through her. "

Was it too early to go home?

"Yes." The brush of Riley's lips against her ear only intensified her desire for the man she'd grown to love more and more over the past month since the night he'd rescued her from her father's place.

"Yes what?" she asked, but knew exactly what he was referring to. His uncanny ability to know exactly what was going through her mind no longer surprised her.

"It's to soon to go home." She squirmed on his lap and smiled when he growled in her ear. "You keep that up and I'll withhold it from you."

Maria leaned back against his chest and trailed her fingers up and down his thigh, smiling when his breath hissed out of him. "Promises. Promises."

Riley bit her ear gently. "Just you wait."

"Ooohhh I'm scared."

"It's a good thing I love you."

"Back at ya, Ash. I love you more than I ever thought I could love anyone else."

Both of Riley's arms closed around her and he kissed the side of her neck. She'd officially moved into his place the night of her abduction. She hadn't wanted to be away from him and he hadn't wanted to be away from her. Her job was going well. The best thing was coming home to someone who would hold her when she needed to be held or be her sounding board when she needed to vent her frustrations away.

Yes, her life was pretty damn good and the man behind her was responsible for it. Maria glanced around the yard at the people congregated in the small space. She'd spent some time with Lily, Grayson's wife, and found she really liked her. Lily's best friend Rita was a bundle of energy, admiring the bevy of handsome men around her, but snuggling into her husband's arms while he kept a watchful eye on their daughter.

Out of the corner of her eye she spied someone standing to the side of the gathering, talking animatedly on his phone.

"What's up with, Italy?" she asked Riley.

A moment of silence passed and she knew her man was watching him. "Don't know."

Maria looked back at Italy and hoped whatever he was going through wasn't because he'd reconnected with his past to help her.

"He'll be fine," Riley said. "Trust the man who loves you.

"I do and I love you, too." Maria cuddled into her lover's embrace and prayed for Italy's troubles to be over.

ABOUT THE AUTHOR

If you enjoyed this book you can subscribe to my newsletter at http://eepurl.com/TZazH to receive notifications about new releases, sales and other pieces of news.

On her very first school report her teacher said 'Nicole likes to tell her own stories'. Many years later she eventually sat down and wrote her first book.

Nicole writes sexy contemporary romances, seducing you one kiss at a time as you turn the pages. She enjoys taking two characters and creating unique situations for them.

Learn more about Nicole Flockton at http://www.nicoleflockton.com.

authornicole@nicoleflockton.com

AVAILABLE NOW

PROTECTING LILY

"Where the hell is my list!"

Lily Green loved lists. Lists made sense. Lists kept her life organized. Lists were pretty. Without her daily to-do list, her day would be an unmitigated disaster. For so many years her lists helped her navigate the rocky social ladder in high school. Helped her during those hard early years of building her business.

Her lists were her crutch. She acknowledged it. She owned it. She wasn't about to change. Without her lists she wouldn't be the CEO of her own company. She wouldn't have money in the bank. More money than she thought she'd ever have. So she'd keep making her lists for the rest of her life. No one would tell her otherwise.

Lily had even made a list for her perfect man.

Every now and then she pulled it out, which was unnecessary as she knew exactly what she'd written on it. Not the clichéd tall dark and handsome, although that would be nice. She didn't want him to be butt ugly, so easy on the eye would be good. Being only five feet two, she didn't want a guy towering over her either. Five feet eight would be the maximum height for her Mr Right.

The most important item on her *perfect man* list would be: nice eyes. Compassionate eyes. Eyes that looked at her with love and desire. To her, eyes were the windows to a person's soul. For too long people's eyes had tricked her. Thinking what she saw in them meant the person cared for her. She knew better now. If a man she met didn't have nice eyes she'd tell him to take a hike. She wanted a kind man. A beta type man. A man who didn't think the world owed him everything. No way would she want an alpha male who wore his arrogance like a winter coat. Her perfect man would be a nice gentle soul who had no issues with her being a list making multi-millionairess.

Lily sighed, one day she'd find the man who matched the items on her list. Until then she would make her daily lists and every day she would cross each item off.

Only she couldn't find today's list. She'd searched

everywhere. She knew she'd made it last night before she'd left the office. It should be sitting in the middle of her desk ready for her to start crossing things off.

"Rita?" She called out to her assistant, anxiety building inside of her as she continued her frantic search.

The door opened and her assistant breezed through the door. "Good morning, Lil. What's up?"

Some days Lily wished she had Rita's carefree attitude. "It's not a good morning. I can't find my list. Have you seen it?"

"Uh no, should I have?"

Lily practically growled when she looked up at Rita. "You were here before me. You came and put—" she paused and picked up a manila folder. "—the photos from yesterday's catalog shoot on my desk. Right in the middle where my list should've been. Only when I picked the folder up my list wasn't underneath. So have you seen it?"

Rita started laughing.

Lily shot her another deadly look. "Remember I can fire you, Rita. Any time I want."

This only made Rita laugh harder. "Lil, there's no way you'd fire me. I'm the only person who puts up with your idiosyncrasies. Your threats don't scare me."

"They should."

"Honey, I've known you too long for anything you say to scare me. Besides we're a team. Have been for a long time. You're stuck with me until our last dying days."

Lily sat down and blew out a long, anxiety cleansing breath. Rita spoke the truth. They'd become friends when they'd both been put into a group home when they'd turned fourteen. Even though they'd gone and done their own thing, the friendship forged during that tough time remained true and strong. When she'd needed an assistant, once her business had taken off, Rita had been the natural choice. Now Rita was married to a nice guy and every day Lily feared Rita walking through the door to announce her pregnancy.

A hand landed on hers, pulling Lily from her thoughts. "You're thinking too hard again, Lil. Yes the day will come, but not for a while and when it does, you'll just convert a spare office into a nursery and hire a nanny so I can keep working with you and have my baby close by."

Lily laughed. She would do exactly that. She'd never been able to hide anything from Rita. Her friend always seemed to know exactly what went through Lily's mind. It made her a great assistant and sometimes an annoying best friend. "Maybe I will, maybe I won't. Depends if you took my list or not."

Rita shook her head and squatted down to look under the desk. "I didn't take your list."

The words were mumbled but Lily heard them anyway. "Well where did it go?"

Rita came out from under the desk and stood. "It's not there, so it didn't fly off and land on the ground when you picked up the folder. Why don't you just write a new one?"

If only it were that easy. She had a routine. A routine she stuck to each and every day. For her day to go the way she wanted, her list had to be written the night before. She placed it right in the middle of her desk ready and waiting for her when she arrived for work the next day. Even the cleaning staff knew not to touch her list.

"Shit, did we have a change in cleaning staff last night?" Lily asked.

Rita lifted a shoulder. "I don't think so."

"But it's possible isn't it?"

"Well yes. But we have a standing instruction that no one is to touch anything on your desk. They're supposed to clean around the edges."

Lily nodded, she always gave the center of her desk a wipe over before writing her list and leaving for the day. She'd done it last night too. She sighed in defeat.

"You know what happens if I have to write a new list, Rita. The day goes to shit."

"Lil," Rita sighed heavily. "It won't go to shit, okay. It only goes to shit because you convince yourself it's going to go to shit. Write your new list and think how disaster free your day is going to be."

Lily reached for her note pad and pen and started writing again, knowing no matter what Rita said, her day wouldn't be smooth. "You keep thinking that, Rita."

"If I didn't love you, Lil, I'd throw my pen at you. Don't forget you've got the appointment with Bent Diamond Company at ten. They want to talk about security while you make the collection for them."

In her list-making zone, Lily nodded. She knew all about the appointment. Had been thinking about how she could let Bent's know she didn't need to have someone watching her twenty four/seven as she worked on the diamond bra collection. While she knew she'd be working with an exorbitant amount of diamonds, she hoped they could come to an agreement which satisfied them both. Working on designs with someone looking over her shoulder gave her the cold sweats. If the company insisted on security, maybe she could get the person to sit outside her workroom.

As she wrote the last item, Lily let out a breath.

Again her list was completed, she could start her day. Although how good it was going to be, only time would tell.

———————

Taking a deep breath Lily walked into the board-room ready to face the executives from Bent Diamond Company. She had no reason to be nervous. They were the ones who approached her to design a collection using their diamonds. They'd given her free reign to design whatever she wanted. The only stipulation they had was that one bra had to be totally covered with diamonds and have one of the large stones as the centerpiece. She had the perfect design for the showstopper piece and prelim-inary designs for the rest of the collection. The purpose of today's meeting was to show them her concepts.

As she looked around the room confidence filled her. She could do this. The men were all older than she expected. Even with their power suits they didn't look threatening at all. Perhaps Rita was right. This day didn't have to be so bad just because her original list went missing.

"Good morning, gentleman I see my assistant has provided each of you with a folder containing my design ideas. Please, take a few moments to look them over."

She paused and waited for them to do as she suggested. She had to stop herself from tapping her pen on the table. Anxiety to hear what they thought of her designs built inside her, bubbling like a piece of Mentos candy in a Coke bottle.

After what seemed endless hours, but was in fact only five minutes at most, the men all looked at her, smiles spread across their faces.

"These designs are stunning," said Paul, the CFO of the company. "You've captured what we're looking for and more."

"Yes indeed," another person spoke.

Lily allowed the compliments to wash over her, pleased with their reactions to her designs. She'd poured over them for hours, working until the lines on the designs blurred and her eyes burned with tiredness.

"I'm pleased you like them. I'm looking forward to receiving the stones to start working on the designs. When were you looking at having the show again?"

People thought because she designed lingerie she could whip bras and panties out in quick succession. No one had any idea how much design went into bras and even panties. The fabric choices had to be well thought out. What may work for a bra, may not work for the matching panties. There would be plenty of fabrics discarded when designing this exclusive collection.

"We are wanting to have the show on Valentines Day."

For once, a client had given her plenty of time to develop her collection. It was only the beginning of November, but taking into account all the holidays, she should be able to have the collection completed by the end of January. Giving her a couple of weeks to finalize model selection and ensure the garments fitted.

"Good, that's plenty of time to guarantee the collection is perfect for you. I have some possible fabric samples, would you like to see them?"

"No," Paul spoke. "We trust your decisions will accentuate our diamonds. Now speaking of diamonds, we understand you will need to have them as soon as possible to enable the stone selection for each garment."

"That's correct," Lily confirmed. "I'm anxious to see them, especially the stone for the finale piece of the collection."

"I think you'll be pleased with the variety of stones provided to you. We'll give you more than you can use so we expect the surplus to be returned to us."

For a fleeting moment indignation filled her at the veiled threat she would keep the unused diamonds. "You can trust me gentleman, I will return the unused stones to you. I have my own business, I'm not going to jeopardize it for a few diamonds."

"We have no doubt you won't return them. But we will be taking an inventory of all the stones we give you—as per our company policy."

"I hope you'll give me a copy of the inventory. At the end of each week I'll email you an updated copy listing the diamonds I've used so you can keep your records up to date as well."

"That sounds good. Now another thing we need to talk about is security."

Lily dreaded this part of the meeting, even though she knew it was coming.

"I'm not sure I'm comfortable having someone watching my every step," Lily told the men in the room. "I like to be alone when I'm working on my designs and as I'm going to have to place the diamonds on the garments to the best advantage I know I'm going to be working all hours. The cost of hiring security is going to be prohibitive to me."

In the back of her mind, she knew she was being unreasonable. Their stance on security made sense. It really did. But she had a system. A system that worked well for her. She didn't do well with changes to her system or her routine. Having security twenty four seven watching her was a huge change.

"This is a non-negotiable part of the deal, Lily. No security then no diamonds."

And her day just went south.

Grayson 'Storm' Warren looked at his laptop screen. He'd really hit rock bottom if he was contemplating opening the email which had just landed in his inbox. He couldn't even believe he'd signed up on that stupid Manservant website. In a moment of drunken weakness he'd let Wayne talk him into signing up. It had seemed like a good idea. Some easy jobs that paid well and gave the company extra income. Now not so much. Now it seemed like the stupidest idea known to mankind.

He should've removed his *profile* the moment he'd sobered up and his hangover had cleared.

The only thing preventing him from deleting the email was the fact he'd looked at his bank account and knew he needed to get an injection of cash. And quick. Staying signed up with a match.com security service company equivalent seemed to be the best way to get some cash. Do a few easy security jobs while waiting to get one of the big contracts he'd submitted proposals on.

Grayson hoped one or two of the contracts would come to fruition. He'd worked hard at keeping the news his former partner had all but fucked up his business quiet and away from prospective clients. But he'd recently missed out on some contracts he'd been sure the company was going to be awarded. Those missed contracts were now hurting him financially.

He tried not to think about what Wayne had done. The way he'd almost killed everything Grayson had spent the last three years building up. He never should've trusted Wayne.

Why had he let Wayne talk him into being in total control of that particular job? He should've taken a look at what was happening. It was Grayson's name and reputation that almost ended up being tarnished. Wayne had fucked off to places unknown with the clients half a million dollars and Grayson had had to use his life savings to ensure the client never knew his money had been stolen.

Grayson had been so stupid. Hadn't listened to his gut when it had told him to watch and check in with Wayne. But he'd been so focused on his own security job, which had gone to hell in hand basket too. If he was looking at employing a security firm he'd bypass his own firm after the shit that had gone down in the last few months.

He was still no closer to finding where Wayne had disappeared to. Sometimes he wondered why he'd ever left the military to start his own company. At least in the military he didn't have to worry about where the next job was going to come from. Being an ex-Seal, he'd never been short of missions. He'd follow the orders given by his team leader. Everything was structured. He never had to stress about where his next influx of cash was going to come from.

Grayson would find Wayne make him pay back the money he took. His business would have its financial security back, and Grayson could plan for his future.

Until then, knowing he had no choice but to accept he was indeed this desperate, he opened the email.

HI GRAYSON,

MY NAME IS RITA KNOWLES AND I WORK FOR LILY GREEN OWNER OF LILY'S LINGERIE. WE ARE IN NEED OF A SECURITY GUARD TO COME AND WORK WITH LILY WHILE SHE DESIGNS A NEW COLLECTION USING DIAMONDS FROM BENT DIAMOND COMPANY. THE COMPANY HAS REQUESTED A SECURITY PRESENCE AT OUR OFFICES. I'VE LOOKED OVER YOUR PROFILE ON THE MANSERVANT SITE AND BELIEVE YOU WILL BE PERFECT FOR THIS JOB.

IF YOU ARE INTERESTED, PLEASE CONTACT ME VIA RETURN EMAIL SO

THAT WE CAN ARRANGE A TIME FOR YOU TO COME TO OUR OFFICE AND DISCUSS OUR REQUIREMENTS WITH YOU.

I LOOK FORWARD TO HEARING FROM YOU SOON.

KIND REGARDS,

RITA KNOWLES

EXECUTIVE ASSISTANT

LILY'S LINGERIE

Grayson read the email twice. He couldn't possibly land a job this important from a website called Manservants.

He composed his email response in his mind wondering if, for once, his life was turning around for the better. If he could land this job and provide a good service, it could be the start to rebuilding his firm and his bank account.

ALSO BY NICOLE FLOCKTON

Guardian Seals Series

Protecting Lily

Protecting Maria

Guarding Erin

Guarding Suzie

Guarding Brielle

The Elite

Fighting to Win

Fighting to Dream

Fighting for Love

Fighting for Redemption

The Freemasons

The Victor

The Hunter

Sweet Texas Secrets

Sweet Texas Fire

Sweet Texas Series Boxed Set

Bound Series

Bound by Her Ring

Bound by His Desire

Bound by Their Love

Bound by The Billionaire's Desire - Boxed Set

Lovers Unmasked Series

Lovers Unmasked: The Complete Series

Masquerade

Rescuing Dawn

Seducing Phoebe

Emerald Springs Legacy Series

Daniel's Decision

Emerald Springs Legacy Collection

Standalone Titles

White Knight (Co-Written with Abigail Owen)

Novellas

Tangled Vines

Melt My Heart Anthology

Tango Love

A Vacation Affair

Medal Up: A Winter Games Duology

Swipe for Mr. Right

Wrong Time for Mr. Right

As you know, this book included at least one character from Susan Stoker's books. To check out more, see below.

Delta Force Heroes Series

Rescuing Rayne (FREE!)
Rescuing Aimee (novella)
Rescuing Emily
Rescuing Harley
Marrying Emily
Rescuing Kassie
Rescuing Bryn
Rescuing Casey
Rescuing Sadie
Rescuing Wendy
Rescuing Mary (Oct 2018)
Rescuing Macie (April 2019)

Badge of Honor: Texas Heroes Series

Justice for Mackenzie (FREE!)
Justice for Mickie
Justice for Corrie
Justice for Laine (novella)
Shelter for Elizabeth
Justice for Boone
Shelter for Adeline

Shelter for Sophie
Justice for Erin
Justice for Milena
Shelter for Blythe
Justice for Hope (Sept 2018)
Shelter for Quinn (Feb 2019)
Shelter for Koren (June 2019)
Shelter for Penelope (Oct 2019)

SEAL of Protection Series

Protecting Caroline (FREE!)
Protecting Alabama
Protecting Fiona
Marrying Caroline (novella)
Protecting Summer
Protecting Cheyenne
Protecting Jessyka
Protecting Julie (novella)
Protecting Melody
Protecting the Future
Protecting Kiera (novella)
Protecting Dakota

SEAL of Protection: Legacy Series

Securing Caite (Jan 2019)
Securing Sidney (May 2019)
Securing Piper (Sept 2019)

Securing Zoey (TBA)
Securing Avery (TBA)
Securing Kalee (TBA)

New York Times, *USA Today* and *Wall Street Journal* Bestselling Author Susan Stoker has a heart as big as the state of Texas where she lives, but this all American girl has also spent the last fourteen years living in Missouri, California, Colorado, and Indiana. She's married to a retired Army man who now gets to follow *her* around the country.

She debuted her first series in 2014 and quickly followed that up with the SEAL of Protection Series, which solidified her love of writing and creating stories readers can get lost in.

If you enjoyed this book, or any book, please consider leaving a review. It's appreciated by authors more than you'll know.

www.stokeraces.com
www.AcesPress.com
susan@stokeraces.com

More Books in the *Special Forces: Operation Alpha World!*

Brynne Asher: Blackburn
Denise Agnew: Dangerous to Hold
Shauna Allen: Awakening Aubrey
Shauna Allen: Defending Danielle
Shauna Allen: Rescuing Rebekah
Shauna Allen: Saving Scarlett
Shauna Allen: Saving Grace
Jennifer Becker: Hiding Catherine
Julia Bright: Saving Lorelei
Victoria Bright: Surviving Savage
Victoria Bright: Going Ghost
Victoria Bright: Jostling Joker
Kendra Mei Chailyn: Beast
Kendra Mei Chailyn: Barbie
Kendra Mei Chailyn : Pitbull
Melissa Kay Clarke: Rescuing Annabeth
Melissa Kay Clarke: Safeguarding Miley
Samantha A. Cole: Handling Haven
Samantha A. Cole: Cheating the Devil
Sue Coletta: Hacked
KaLyn Cooper: Rescuing Melina
Liz Crowe: Marking Mariah
Jordan Dane: Redemption for Avery

Jordan Dane: Fiona's Salvation
Riley Edwards: Protecting Olivia
Riley Edwards: Redeeming Violet
Nicole Flockton: Protecting Maria
Nicole Flockton: Guarding Erin
Nicole Flockton: Guarding Suzie
Nicole Flockton: Guarding Brielle
Casey Hagen: Shielding Nebraska
Casey Hagen: Shielding Harlow
Casey Hagen: Shielding Josie
Desiree Holt: Protecting Maddie
Kathy Ivan: Saving Sarah
Kathy Ivan: Saving Savannah
Kathy Ivan: Saving Stephanie
Jesse Jacobson: Protecting Honor
Jesse Jacobson: Fighting for Honor
Jesse Jacobson: Defending Honor
Jesse Jacobson: Summer Breeze
Silver James: Rescue Moon
Silver James: SEAL Moon
Silver James: Assassin's Moon
Becca Jameson: Saving Sofia
Kate Kinsley: Protecting Ava
Heather Long: Securing Arizona
Heather Long: Guarding Gertrude
Heather Long: Protecting Pilar
Heather Long: Covering Coco

Kirsten Lynn: Joining Forces for Jesse
Margaret Madigan: Bang for the Buck
Margaret Madigan: Buck the System
Margaret Madigan: Jungle Buck
Margaret Madigan: December Chill
Rachel McNeely: The SEAL's Surprise Baby
Rachel McNeely: The SEAL's Surprise Bride
KD Michaels: Saving Laura
KD Michaels: Protecting Shane
Wren Michaels: The Fox & The Hound
Wren Michaels: The Fox & The Hound 2
Wren Michaels: Shadow of Doubt
Wren Michaels: Shift of Fate
Wren Michaels: Steeling His Heart
Kat Mizera: Protecting Bobbi
Mary B Moore: Force Protection
LeTeisha Newton: Protecting Butterfly
LeTeisha Newton: Protecting Goddess
LeTeisha Newton: Protecting Vixen
LeTeisha Newton: Protecting Heartbeat
MJ Nightingale: Protecting Beauty
MJ Nightingale: Betting on Benny
MJ Nightingale: Protecting Secrets
Sarah O'Rourke: Saving Liberty
Debra Parmley: Protecting Pippa
Lainey Reese: Protecting New York
Jenika Snow: Protecting Lily

Jen Talty: Burning Desire

Jen Talty: Burning Kiss

Jen Talty: Burning Skies

Jen Talty: Burning Lies

Megan Vernon: Protecting Us

Megan Vernon: Protecting Earth

Made in the USA
Middletown, DE
05 February 2023